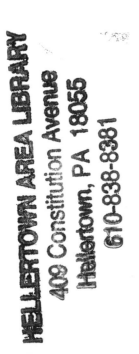

THERE'S NO WIFI
ON THE PRAIRIE

IN DUE TIME

THERE'S NO WIFI ON THE PRAIRIE

by Nicholas O. Time

SIMON SPOTLIGHT

New York   London   Toronto   Sydney   New Delhi

SIMON SPOTLIGHT
An imprint of Simon & Schuster Children's Publishing Division
1230 Avenue of the Americas, New York, New York 10020
This Simon Spotlight hardcover edition July 2016
Copyright © 2016 by Simon & Schuster, Inc.
Text by Sheila Sweeny Higginson. Cover illustration by Stephen Gilpin.
All rights reserved, including the right of reproduction in whole or in part in any form. SIMON SPOTLIGHT and colophon are registered trademarks of Simon & Schuster, Inc. For information about special discounts for bulk purchases, please contact Simon & Schuster Special Sales at 1-866-506-1949 or business@simonandschuster.com.
Designed by Jay Colvin. The text of this book was set in Adobe Garamond Pro.
Manufactured in the United States of America 1216 FFG
10 9 8 7 6 5 4 3 2 1
ISBN 978-1-4814-8232-5 (hardcover)
ISBN 978-1-4814-8231-8 (paperback)
ISBN 978-1-4814-8233-2 (eBook)
Library of Congress Control Number 2016957833

CHAPTER	TITLE
1	Don't Have a Cow

I like hanging out in the library after school, even though I don't study. I don't *need* to study, which I know sounds obnoxious, but I'm just really lucky. I inherited my mom's "elephant" memory. (That's what she calls it—she hears or sees something once and then remembers it forever; and there's an old expression that says "an elephant never forgets.") So if I just listen in class and do my homework, I never have to actually sit down and study. Unlike my friend Ethan, who is sitting across from me right now, labeling the parts of a cell and doing it mostly wrong.

I sigh and continue playing MineFarm on my phone. I can correct him in a minute. A few weeks ago Ethan asked me to tutor him after school, which I agreed to do, not only because he's a really good friend but also because the library is *quiet*, unlike my house, so being here is actually pleasant.

Ethan passes me his paper to look over, and I point out where he's mixed up different parts, as well as spelled mitochondria wrong.

Ethan groans. "Ava, if I didn't like you so much, I'd really *dis*like you. You get straight A's and you don't do *anything* to earn them."

"I know," I say. "I'm sorry. But I can't help having an elephant memory. Plus, I have my phone, so anything I *don't* know, I can just look up, and poof! There it is. Technology is a wonderful thing."

I bring my eyes back to my phone, where some zombies have gotten loose in my MineFarm game and are eating all of my cows. Shoot! I'll have to steal some of Ethan's cows, I guess. He always takes really good care of his farm. He's probably one of the best gamers I've ever played with.

Ethan must hear the sound of my cows being eaten because he pipes up, "Ava, don't even think about stealing my cows."

"Um, okay." I start to do it anyway.

Ethan is rewriting "mitochondria." "How'd you get this elephant memory anyway? Can I buy one at the mall?"

I smile. "Doubt it. I got it from my mom. When she was younger, she got into a really fancy college out in California but didn't end up going because she wanted to stay close to home. I can't believe it! If I had the chance to move to sunny California, I'd be there in a minute."

"To be closer to your dad?" Ethan asks.

My parents are divorced and my dad lives in Los Angeles now. My mom and my younger twin sisters and baby brother and I live here on the east coast, and my mom works full-time, so there are always babysitters and missed meals and messes and laundry. Ugh. My house is a disaster. My dad lives alone and has a housekeeper, so when I go see him, it's like heaven.

"I'd like to live in California partly because of

my dad, I guess," I tell Ethan. "But also because life is just *nicer* there. Haven't you seen the TV shows? It's warm and sunny all year, and there's less stress. Everyone is just hanging out outside. Everyone is happy there. It's the place to be."

I manage to steal about six of Ethan's cows, one at a time, and put them in my MineFarm cow pen. I turn the volume down on my phone so he doesn't hear me.

"I know what you just did," Ethan says as he starts to pack up his homework. "And you're cheating yourself, you know."

"Huh? I don't know what you're talking about," I say innocently.

"Stealing my cows! The fun of the game is in working hard and building your farm from scratch. And keeping it going, bit by bit, every day. But you just skip all that and take my animals. It's called *Mine*Farm, not *Yours*Farm."

Ethan laughs to himself, and I can't help laughing along with him. He knows me so well. It's nice to have a friend who will let you steal his cows and then really not even care about it. *And* make stupid jokes about it.

As I'm looking at Ethan, I see something *very weird* out the window behind him. It's an actual cow. Like, a *real*, live cow. And it's looking at me.

I start laughing *really* hard. "Hey, Ethan. Don't have a cow, but—"

Ethan shakes his head. "I'm *not* having a cow. I'm actually being very cool about the fact that you constantly steal supplies from me and I still play with you."

"No, no," I say. "Look, there's a cow right there, out the window! In the school yard! A real cow!" I point over his head, and Ethan turns around and sees it.

"That is a real dairy cow," Ethan says. "Holy cow. Holy COW! And is that . . . ?"

I nod my head. Not that it wasn't already weird enough, but our school's librarian, Ms. Tremt, is now outside patting the cow and trying to lead it away from the front of the school.

"I'm going to go help her!" Ethan says, jumping up. He runs toward the side exit door of the library and is outside in just a moment. I can't believe what I'm seeing, but it looks like Ms. Tremt and Ethan are talking to the cow, trying to verbally convince it to go somewhere. Of course, it looks like it weighs about two tons, so good luck to them.

Ethan looks through the window at me and throws up his hands. He clearly thinks Ms. Tremt is a bit batty. Then he tries clapping and calling to the cow like he would call to a dog. Surprise, surprise—that doesn't work either.

I shake my head at their ridiculousness and do a quick search on "how to move a cow" on my phone. Technology. Seriously. It's the best.

The answer pops up in less than three seconds, and I start digging in my lunch bag for my leftovers. As soon as I have something in my hand, I go outside and walk straight up to the cow.

I can hear Ms. Tremt talking now. "What if somebody sees you?" she tells the cow. "You could fall into the wrong hands! You can't just take the situation into your own hooves, you know."

I give the cow a piece of the carrot I'm holding, then begin walking away, holding the rest of the carrot. The cow follows me, as easy as one, two, three. Thanks, Internet! You've saved the day, for the billionth time.

"Well done, Ava," Ms. Tremt says. "You have a real way with animals. Now, could you please lead your new friend into the back room of the library for me?"

I look from her to Ethan and back to her. "Uh, Ms. Tremt? Shouldn't we call animal control or something? Or the ASPCA? Or, um, a vet? My mom is a vet. I could call her."

Ms. Tremt smiles broadly at me, then uses her lime-green fuzzy scarf to point in the direction of the side door to the library. "That won't be necessary, Ava. But thank you for your suggestions. Just take Ms. Cow to the back room."

I do as she asks, because even a kooky grown-up is still a grown-up, but I exchange more than a few looks with Ethan while doing it. All I can think about is how big of a mess that cow is going to make when it goes to the bathroom in the middle of the school's library. Maybe Ethan and I will have to study at his house tomorrow after school.

As soon as the cow is settled in the back room with Ms. Tremt, I go to gather up my things. My phone beeps that it's five thirty p.m., and I realize how late I've stayed. "I've got to get home," I tell Ethan.

He nods and helps me pack up. "Oh yeah! I forgot it was your big night, right?"

I roll my eyes. "My big night" is just the night that my mom's and my favorite TV show, *World's Weirdest Animals*, comes on. "Exactly. So I need to jet. Are you coming?"

Ethan shakes his head. "Nah, not yet. Ms. Tremt asked me to come to her office and help her with something real quick before I go. But I'll see you later on MineFarm. I've got to start breeding more cows, apparently."

I laugh and wave good-bye, then head out the side door again, this time to the bike rack where my scooter is locked up. There are a few kids grabbing bikes, and I wait a moment before I push in to get my scooter.

Once I have it unlocked, I send a quick text to my mom to let her know I'm leaving school and will be home in seven minutes. As I'm sliding my phone into my backpack, someone slams into me, and a bunch of my homework papers explode out of my bag and fly all over the ground.

Ugh! I guess I forgot to zip it up. I do that sometimes. I bend to pick them up, and as I do, I see it was a Viking—yes, a *Viking*—that slammed into me. He's wearing metal armor and a horned helmet and everything.

"Um, hello?" I say.

He grunts, and to my surprise, starts helping me to pick up the papers. He hands me a stack, then says, "Many hands make light work."

Quick as lightning, I put the two very weird things that have happened that day together. "You wouldn't happen to own a cow, would you?" I ask.

He narrows his eyes. "Yes, I do. In fact, all cows are my cows."

Hmm. This just got weirder. I decide to leave the, uh, *Viking* and the cow situation in Ms. Tremt's capable hands. I figure she'll know what to do. Weird things always seem to be happening in the library and around Ms. Tremt, now that I think about it. I turn back to the Viking. "Um, okay. Gotta go!"

I hop on my scooter and sail home. Hopefully it will be less chaotic than it was in the library this afternoon. But I doubt it.

9

CHAPTER	TITLE
2	Dinner Disaster

My scoot home is one of my favorite parts of my day. It's the calm before the storm, so to speak. This time of year, the sun is still shining, the breeze is cool on my face, and I am blissfully alone.

Then I reach my house and have to go inside.

As soon I as walk in, I can tell it's one of *those days*. There are piles of stuff everywhere. My twin sisters' backpacks are blocking the door. There's a line of shoes from the living room to the kitchen. A basket of folded laundry has been sitting on the couch for two days, but no one has put it away.

"Hello?" I call.

"In here!" Mom calls back cheerfully. I can hear a note of strain beneath the cheer though.

I hang up my backpack and jacket and put my shoes in the shoe cubby. Then I step over the trail of my siblings' stuff and make my way to the kitchen.

Mom is unpacking the lunch boxes, so I hand her mine and take a seat on a stool at the counter. There's nothing cooking on the stove and I don't smell any good smells in the air. I do detect a hint of dirty diaper from my baby brother, Adam, who's in the playpen in the corner.

"Shouldn't dinner be ready, Mom? We only have, like, twelve minutes until our show starts," I remind her.

Normally Mom tries to feed the younger kids earlier on Tuesdays, so that she and I can eat together and watch *World's Weirdest Animals*. It's the only time she and I get to do anything alone. Ever.

"We're behind today, Ava," Mom explains. "I had to stay to help with a patient, and the babysitter took the kids to the park, so everyone has just gotten home."

I groan. I can't help it. I know it's rude, but I was at school all day and I'm hungry and tired.

"You know," Mom says, still managing to sound mostly cheerful but with an impatient edge now, "if you'd *help* me, I could get things going a lot faster."

"Ummm," I say. I know I should help. But there's so *much* that needs to be done. The messes, the laundry, the baby. It's overwhelming. Where would I even start? Besides, isn't that Mom's job? To take care of us? I'm still a kid too! I just happen to be slightly older than the other ones who live here. "I guess I could," I say grudgingly.

Adam starts wailing in his playpen, and I'm afraid Mom will make me grab him and change his diaper, but my sisters, Tania and Tess, come in and get him. They're only in third grade, but they're pretty helpful. Maybe because there're two of them.

Mom starts some water boiling in a pot and pulls out a box of spaghetti and a jar of sauce. "I guess this is dinner," she says with a sigh. "You could make a salad," she suggests to me.

Ugh. I hate washing all those vegetables. Mom makes me wash everything *really carefully* because of pesticides. It takes forever.

"Umm," I say again. I'm pretty good at not saying *No, I won't help* but not getting up and actually helping.

Our dog, Sunny, is following Mom around, like all animals do, and Mom accidentally steps back on him and trounces on his front paw.

Sunny yelps and limps away. Exasperated, cheerfulness gone, Mom glares at me. "Ava Marie, either help me get dinner on the table or take the dog out. But do *something* before I lose my mind. Please."

"I'll take Sunny out," I say quickly. Walking Sunny is my favorite chore, because it's outside, it's quiet, and because Sunny doesn't wear diapers or wipe sticky fingers on me or steal my head-bands. He might be my favorite family member, in fact.

I hop up and retrieve Sunny's leash from the hook by the door (one of the only things in the house that's in its proper place, because

I'm the one who hung it there). "Here, boy!" I call, and Sunny comes running. I glance at the clock as we're heading outside. "Only two minutes till the show starts, Mom! We've never missed it . . ."

Mom throws me a look that's like a bucket of icy water. Something tells me this may be the night we miss the show. But Mom is usually able to ride the waves of chaos around here without getting stressed. It's one of her best qualities. Whereas I get totally overwhelmed and escape.

I hop on my scooter, and Sunny and I head down the sidewalk together. Sunny doesn't mind if I scoot while we walk, because he's that sweet of a dog. He's just happy to be outside and free. It's so nice out, in fact, that I decide we should go around the whole block.

"Let's not go back right away, Sunny," I tell him. "See if they miss us."

I know that I'm grumpy because I'm hungry, but I'm also bummed I'll be missing my one-on-one time with my mom. Watching our show is really all we get, because Mom is so busy working full-time at the emergency vet clinic and taking care of the four of us (five, if you count Sunny). I had to *ask* just to get her to agree to make *World's Weirdest Animals* our special thing every week, because Mom doesn't even have time to *realize* that we don't get alone time together. She probably wouldn't even have thought about it.

I pull up MineFarm on my phone to see if Ethan has started rebuilding his cow population yet. But he isn't there. That's odd. He usually spends a lot of time on MineFarm in the evening, because he says it's the best time for him to concentrate on his crops. I text him to see what's up, but he doesn't answer.

I look at the time and realize my show has already started. *Grrr.* Luckily, I have the app for our cable company on my phone, so I can manage the kid controls for my brother and sisters, and I can also set the DVR to record the show. I do that quickly, so Mom and I can at least watch it later, maybe, when everyone else is in bed. Again, technology rules!

The app then shows me its main page, which has news from the cable company. One of the headings catches my eye.

*OPEN CASTING CALL! KIDS
AGES 10–14!!*

*Do you have a flair for the
dramatic? Have you always
imagined yourself being on TV
and living in California? Can you
memorize things quickly and easily?
If so, you might be the star of our
next big show! Please join us for
an open-call audition for our new
tween hit,* Sunny Days in L.A.*! We
want to meet you!*

I think my jaw literally drops. This audition was *made* for me. I can memorize scripts! I can live in L.A.! I can be a huge TV star and live the good life!

"Sunny, should I audition for a TV show and move to California and live with my dad? Wouldn't that be soooooo nice? You can come with me. I'll be able to afford fancy dog treats *and* a fancy new scooter for myself."

Sunny looks up at me, his ears perked. He

looks like he's thinking it over. I take that as a yes.

"I think I should do it. I can make it to the audition after school tomorrow, no problem. We've got a school field trip in the afternoon, and then I'll just scoot over to the cable company's offices and show them how quickly I can learn lines. What should I *wear*, though? That's the real problem."

Mentally, I begin to scroll through my wardrobe, hoping I can think of something that screams "TV star."

I'm thinking so hard I steer my scooter directly into a *cow*. On the *sidewalk*!

"Mooooooooooo," says the cow. It blinks at me, all friendly and happy, and noses at my hand for a treat. It's the same cow from earlier. It's got to be. But didn't I leave it in the back room of the library?

Now it's just standing on the sidewalk, blocking our path. Sunny barks at the cow, and the cow moos back and looks at me adoringly. But I have no time for dealing with cows right now, no matter how friendly they may be. The cow will just have to find its own way home.

"Something's *weird* around here," I say. "C'mon, Sunny. Let's get home for dinner."

As we come in the back door, I hang up Sunny's leash. Tania and Tess are at the kitchen table, finishing their spaghetti. I must have been gone longer than I thought. Probably because I was thinking about my TV audition.

"Where are Mom and Adam?" I ask.

Tania gets up to clear her plate and put it in the sink. "Adam had a tantrum, so Mom put him in the bathtub and now she's trying to rock him to sleep. She hasn't eaten yet."

Tess gets up to join her. "We've got to take our showers now and do homework. Mom said so. You probably do too."

I ignore this last part.

"Yeah, okay, good night," I tell my sisters. I fix myself a plate of the already cold spaghetti and head into the living room. At least I recorded the show so Mom and I can watch it when she comes down. In the meantime, I can watch my favorite trivia show and eat.

Sometime later, I feel Mom shake me awake. The TV is still on with the volume way down, but the lamps are off and it's pitch-black outside.

"Ava, honey, go up to bed," Mom says.

"What? Did I fall asleep? I was waiting for you to come down so we could watch our show. I recorded it."

Mom sighs. "I'm sorry, Ava. It took me forever to settle Adam, and then I had to help the twins with their homework and read to them. And I had to clean up the kitchen. But it's ten o'clock now, and you have school tomorrow. So please go up to bed."

"Mom," I say. I want to complain. I wanted our time together. But I also know my mom is exhausted. So I stop myself.

"Ava, I'm very sorry we didn't get to watch our show together," she says, sounding defeated. "I look forward to it too, you know."

If that were true, wouldn't she have made time for *me*? She made time to take care of everyone else. Maybe I really should audition for this TV show. After all, no one would miss me here. I might as well be a big star in California and live with my dad. Then I can send some money home, to help with my little sisters and brother.

I stumble upstairs to change and brush my

teeth. Once I'm in bed, I check my phone and see that Ethan has done some work on MineFarm. Good. I was worried about him. And even more worried I wouldn't have a place to steal farm animals from if the zombies return.

I text Ethan: *I have big news! Need your help tomorrow.*

He texts back right away: *Me too. Wear comfortable shoes.*

At the end of his message is an alarm clock emoji. What is that? Is he reminding me to set my alarm for school?

I check my phone alarm to see that it's set, and it is. For the hundredth time I realize how I really couldn't live without this phone. It's my whole life. It's more reliable than my own mother sometimes!

I put the pillow over my head and close my eyes. After all, TV stars need their beauty sleep.

CHAPTER	TITLE
3	Anagrams

M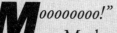*ooooooooo!"*

My head pops up and I scan the hallway at school. Is that a cow? *Again?*

"Mooooooooo!"

There's no cow in sight, but I quickly realize my hip pocket is vibrating. Someone has reset the text message alert sound on my phone to a cow mooing. It has to have been Ethan. He loves doing that kind of thing.

I check my phone and see that he's sent me a picture of a basketball in the library, with the words *Meet me here, right now!*

"What?" I exclaim. We're supposed to be boarding the bus for our field trip at the front of the school in a few minutes. Why would he want me to meet him in the library? And come to think of it, why was he acting so weird at lunch? I tried to tell him about my audition later today and he just kept nodding and smiling at me with this funny look on his face, and when I asked what was up, he said, "You'll see."

I assume he's planning a massive MineFarm raid on my cows (his former cows), so I've been checking in, but nothing's happened.

I decide to cruise by the library on the way to the bus, just to see why he's acting like such a weirdo. If I hurry, I can still make it on time.

As I walk in, Ms. Tremt comes straight toward me and looks me over. "Oh, good," she says. "You're wearing comfortable shoes. That's every traveler's number one mistake, you know."

"Huh?" I ask. "It's just a field trip to a farmers' market."

"Moooooooo!"

Ms. Tremt whirls around. "No!" she yells. "Bad

bovine! I just got you back home, and you *know* this whole thing needs to go according to plan!"

Wow. This lady is all kinds of kooky. I pull my phone out of my pocket and show it to her. *"Mooooooooo!"* it says again.

"Sorry, Ms. Tremt," I say. "It's just my phone mooing. Ethan set it like that, and I forgot to turn it off."

Ms. Tremt looks relieved. "I see. Well, that won't be a problem today! Come with me. Opportunity is knocking." She leans in close to me. "And when opportunity knocks, we don't want to keep it waiting," she says knowingly.

Even when she's not chasing a cow around, Ms. Tremt is a little odd.

"Yeah, um, okay," I say. I check my phone again to see what my new message is. It's my mom telling me she's got to work late again this evening and that the babysitter will stay with the little kids and order dinner for everyone, so I don't have to rush home.

I'm happy I'll still be able to go to the audition, but that means another night of chaos when I do get home.

"You know," says Ms. Tremt. "You're really not supposed to use your phone at school, Ava."

"Yeah, I know. I'm sorry." I'm about to explain it was a text from my mom, when Ethan suddenly appears from the back room of the library. He looks wildly excited and kind of sweaty. He rushes toward me.

"Ava! You're here!" he says. "I've been dying to tell you my news *all day*, but Ms. Tremt said I had to wait until now."

"Tell me what?" Silently I hope it isn't another story about a loose dairy cow in the library. Or what the dairy cow *did* in the back room of the library. *Ewww.*

"I traveled back in time and played basketball with *Michael Jordan* in game six of the 1998 finals last night! I couldn't take a photo of the game because Ms. Tremt has all these rules. . . ."

Ms. Tremt gives him a look, and he stops cold. A second later, she nods at him to continue. It's like a weird puppeteering trick or something.

"Anyway, now it's *your* turn, Ava!" says Ethan. "Where do you want to go?"

"Where do I want to go?" I repeated. "I have

no idea what you're talking about, but yes, it *is* my turn for once! I'm totally going to change my own life today," I say. "But I already told you about that at lunch. So what's going on?"

"Ava, this will come as a shock, so prepare yourself," Ms. Tremt says gently, looking at me as if I might bolt.

I don't. I stand still and listen. I'm not really expecting our librarian to have earth-shattering news. Ms. Tremt takes a deep breath. When she begins speaking again, she speaks slowly and clearly, as if she wants to be certain I hear every single word.

"Ethan traveled to the past last night, and I helped him," Ms. Tremt continues. "I thought he deserved a reward for all of the studying he's been doing. And since I know you've been helping him—"

"Or trying to help," interrupts Ethan. "In between letting zombies eat my MineFarm cows. And letting me label the parts of a cell wrong and then correcting me after I've finished the whole thing and have to erase it all and start over."

I shrug. "You needed to learn it."

"*Anyway*, as your reward for helping him, now it's *your* turn," says Ms. Tremt. She fluffs her purple scarf just so around her neck and hands me a large leather book. It has fancy gold gilded pages and beautiful lettering on the cover that reads, *The Book of Memories*.

"What's this?" I ask. "I don't have time to read a book, Ms. Tremt. Ethan and I have to board the bus for our field trip, like, *now*."

"Just listen, Ava!" Ethan says, his eyes shining.

"You've been helping your friend study, and now you get to reap the benefits," says Mrs. Tremt. "Hard work always has its rewards, Ava. Remember that."

"Um, great," I say, still totally confused. Why is Ethan hopping around like a happy bunny, and why is Ms. Tremt being so pushy with this book? "Ethan, we've got to *go*," I say again.

Ethan shakes his head. "Stop, Ava, and *listen*. We're going to travel to the past. Ms. Tremt's name—*Valerie Tremt*—is an anagram for 'time traveler,'" he says. "She's a *time traveler*!"

"And *my* name is an anagram for . . ." I think for a moment. What's an anagram for Ava Larsen?

26

"'Alas Raven,' but you don't see me flapping my wings around the room," I joke. "C'mon. Let's *go.*"

Ms. Tremt and Ethan don't laugh. I admit, I was expecting a little laugh. After all, "Alas Raven" is pretty good.

"Take this seriously," Ms. Tremt says, shaking a finger at me.

Meanwhile, Ethan looks like he's trying to do anagrams in his head. "Um, mine would be 'Thean,' or 'Thane.' Naw, those aren't good. . . ."

"Are you two feeling okay?" I take out my phone to check the time.

"Ava!" Ethan snaps. "Listen, all the weird stuff that happens at school . . . the cow, that Viking guy you told me about?"

"Yeah, this school is totally weird. That's why I've decided to become a child actor and move to L.A.," I say.

"Ava, I know you think living in California would be cool, but trust me, this is way cooler! Just think for a second. If you could go back in time to change one little thing in the past, what would it be?"

I think for a second. "Easy. I'd make my

mom decide to go to college in California like she should have back in 1991, so I could be living the sweet life now," I declare. "Then, even if my parents still ended up getting divorced, my dad would be nearby, and we'd have a pool."

"I don't think that will work . . . ," says Ethan, looking disappointed.

"Nope, totally fine!" says Ms. Tremt. "Quick, let's do this, before that cow comes back. She's been surprisingly uncooperative this whole time. . . ."

"What? Ms. Tremt, I thought you said you couldn't change the past for selfish reasons. . . . Time travel works via positive energy, right?" says Ethan.

"No, no, no, noooooo," says Ms. Tremt, giving a little laugh. "I didn't say that. He's remembering wrong." She starts nervously motioning toward me for some reason. Maybe because I'm filming the two of them and their total weirdness on my phone.

"You guys are hilarious," I say as I film. "Did you arrange this skit just for me?"

"You told me I couldn't change the outcome of the playoff game," Ethan grumbles, mostly to himself. "Because that would be selfish. That's what you *said.*"

"Ava, delete that video, put the phone down, and come here," says Ms. Tremt. Her voice has stopped being light and silly and instead is more firm and commanding than I've ever heard it before. Immediately I do as she asks.

"I'm sorry, Ms. Tremt," I say. "I wasn't going to post the video anywhere. You guys were just being too funny, talking about time travel and positive energy and stuff, I just wanted to get you both on film so I could rewatch it later. It was hilarious!"

"Ava, I can't seem to get through to you, which isn't surprising, but you'll believe me when you arrive," Ms. Tremt says. "Now, both of you wear these scarves, because they'll not only make you blend in where you're going, but they also make it possible for you to easily communicate with people who speak other languages. They're sort of like your visual and audio camouflage."

"Uh, great!" I say, deciding to play along. I need to get out of here and get on the bus. The scarf is actually really cute, though. It's pink and orange stripes, and it might look good at my audition later. It would make me stand out from the other kids auditioning. "People make fun of your style, Ms. Tremt, but I like your scarves."

"Thank you," says Ms. Tremt. "So, what's your final decision, then, your mom's childhood home, 1991? That's where you want to go?"

Still playing along, I nod and say, "Yep, sure."

Ms. Tremt writes it down carefully in the unusual-looking *Book of Memories.* Her pen begins to glow oddly. The whole thing makes me feel like I've stumbled into one of my favorite sci-fi TV shows.

Ethan grins at me. "When the pen glows, it means it's working."

I watch as *The Book of Memories* begins to grow as large as pair of French doors. It must be some trick, like a projected image or something. That would be just like Ethan.

"Seriously, this is the best prank anyone has ever played on me," I tell him.

"It's not a prank," he replies, but the grin is still on his face.

Suddenly I look around and ask, "Are you filming this? Am I going to be on TV, like

30

those hidden-camera shows? Awesome."

"You have three hours in the past," says Ms. Tremt, talking right over me. "Ethan, you know how to return, right?"

"The book will glow when we have a ten-minute warning. We write today's date and time in the book and let it grow," says Ethan, putting on a watch that Ms. Tremt gives him. "Then we step into the book and back into the present. But we must do it right then or we'll be stuck in the past forever."

"And?" prompts Ms. Tremt.

"And we need to watch out for other time travelers," Ethan says, fiddling with the watch.

I roll my eyes.

"Right, very good." Then Ms. Tremt says to me, "Don't worry, dear. Everything will make sense . . . in due time." She whispers, "Don't forget your phone," as she tucks the phone into my pocket.

Ethan grabs my hand and yanks me forward in a flying leap into the book, shouting, "1991, here we come!"

BOOMF!

"*Moo!*"

Is that my phone?

"*Moo!*"

Why am I all wet, and . . . smelly? And why can't I *see*?

"*Moo!*"

I've got to answer my phone. Where is my phone? It could be my mom worried about getting home late tonight. And I've got to tell her I might be late because I'm doing that audition.

There's something slimy and rancid on my face, and I wipe at my eyes with my sleeve to clear them. I can't imagine what this slime is, but it looks like . . . slop? Whatever it is, it's gross.

"Moo!"

Where is my phone?

Something licks my face. It feels like my dog, Sunny, only it's a *much* bigger tongue. I'm finally able to look up and see . . . a cow. Yes, a real cow. Again. And it's the *cow* that's mooing insistently at me and not my phone.

But what's even weirder is that I'm lying on a broken fence, with slats of wood poking me in the back, and my shoulder is in a broken pig trough. A pig trough?

I scream. Then I scream again.

"Stop screaming!" Ethan whispers in my ear. He's beside me, also half inside the trough, only I didn't notice because he's covered in the pig slop too. He looks and smells disgusting.

"My head hurts," he complains. "Why did Tremt have to drop us someplace so *hard*. A feather bed would have been nice. Or a trampoline."

"What are you talking about? *Drop* us? Why aren't we on the bus to the farmers' market?" I'm shrieking, but quietly, since he told me not to yell and I don't want to upset the gigantic cow still inches from my face.

"*We've traveled to the past*, Ava. We told you, like, fifteen times that that's what we were going to do. And now we're here. You're going to love it. I promise." He rubs his temples. "Although, seriously, I would have picked a more exciting place to travel back to than a farm. And how come you never told me your mom grew up in the Midwest?"

"She didn't. And who says we're in the Midwest?"

I look around, wondering if I should believe him. It does look like we're on some sort of prairie. There's nothing but blue skies, fields of tall grasses, and a large cornfield beside us. And, of course, the fence we're lying on and a sod-covered stable beside it.

"We didn't time travel," I say stubbornly. "I've never seen this field before in my life, and my mom grew up in Connecticut. This is *not* my grandparents' house."

"Hmm, well, maybe we landed in the wrong place," Ethan says. "Time travel is funny. Ms. Tremt told me it's powered by positive energy, which is unpredictable and confusing . . . like that cow. Why does that cow love you so much?"

The cow is licking my shoulder to get more of the slops. It's being very gentle though, and when it pulls back to look me in the face, I swear its eyes are smiling. I give it a quick pat on the nose and it looks back at me lovingly. It's got to be the same cow that was outside my house last night and in the library yesterday. And I have *got* to be dreaming.

"Ethan, I want you to swear to me right now that this is really happening and we're not on a hidden-camera show. Because if all this ends with me being very famous, then it'll be worth it. But if not, I'm really, really mad."

"Don't be mad! It's not a show, though. We're in the past, only I don't know where." Ethan stands up and offers me a hand. "Let's look around. The sooner we figure things out, the better."

"We really destroyed this fence," I say, rubbing

my backside as I stand up. We landed right on the thing and brought down two long sections. About a hundred yards away, I see a beautiful chestnut-brown horse grazing. The air smells like the sweet prairie grasses, and the ground is so flat it seems like I can see for miles. Only there's nothing to see! Just prairie. Not a road. Not a sign. Nothing.

There is a small wooden house a few hundred feet to our right. It looks more like a cabin really, with two windows roughly cut into the wood and tar paper instead of shingles on the roof. And beyond the house, closer to where the cornfields begin, is an old-timey plow.

Something clicks.

"Ethan," I whisper. "I don't think—"

I'm cut off by the sound of a woman's voice. Quickly Ethan and I duck behind the trough, even though it isn't much of a cover.

"Come here, chicky chickens," says the voice. It sounds like it has a Scandinavian accent. I look around for the speaker, but she must be on the other side of the house. "Time for your feed," she calls. Then I hear something being scattered around and lots of squawking.

A minute later I see the woman walking into the house. Her hair is pinned up in a braid that's wrapped around the crown of her head, and she's in a long, old-timey calico dress and apron. She looks like she's in a play.

"Uh-oh," says Ethan, hunching down further behind the trough. "This feels wrong."

"Yeah, you think? This isn't Connecticut in 1991!"

I look around some more, thinking. I study the old-timey laundry hanging on a clothesline. Then there's the plow, which I recognize from a book. Then, through the open window of the house, I hear the woman call out, "Martha! Martha Pedersen, it's time to husk the corn!"

Martha Pedersen . . . did I really just hear that?

My jaw drops, and Ethan turns to look at me. My mom has mentioned that name to me before. It's my great-great-great grandmother.

"Ethan!" I say, doing the math. "This isn't 1991. It's *1891*! And we're out in the prairies of Minnesota!"

"No *way*! That's awesome!"

I start to shake my head and explain that uh,

no, that is *not* awesome, when suddenly, I hear a man's voice. He yells, "WHAT HAPPENED TO THE FENCE? LAURA, KIDS, COME OUT HERE AND LOOK AROUND—THERE MUST BE HORSE THIEVES NEARBY!"

I look at Ethan with wide eyes. His eyes are just as wide as mine, which confirms what I'm thinking: We're in big trouble.

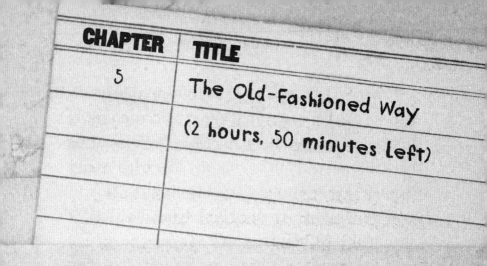

Yup, big trouble. Ethan and I broke the fence (thanks, Ms. Tremt!), and since we happen to be the only people in what looks to be about a thousand-mile radius, we're the ones who'll be accused of being horse thieves!

My mind starts racing, trying to remember everything I learned in history class about life on the prairie back in the 1800s. Didn't they throw horse thieves in jail back in 1891? Who knew I'd have to remember all this stuff one day to save my neck on the Minnesota prairies?

Panicked, I look at Ethan. Why did he do this to us? He knew that the stupid time-travel book was real! And he let Ms. Tremt send us back in time without having any idea what would happen! I've got to get away from him. He's in cahoots with Ms. Tremt. He's paying me back for stealing his MineFarm cows!

Instinctively, I spring to my feet and start running away from him, straight for the cornfields. It's the only available place to hide around here, as there seem to be no trees and I'm pretty sure they'd find me hiding behind the petticoats on the laundry clothesline.

My feet pound against the grass. I'm hoping to make it to the tall stalks of corn before the family—my ancestors!—see me. I've got to get to a safe spot so I can look up the GPS on my phone and figure out how to get home. Maybe I can take an Uber.

I hear an ominous thudding behind me and look nervously over my shoulder, only to see that the *cow* is following me. Honestly. Does it contain the spirit of a dead relative or something? Why does it like me so much? I mean, I appreciate it, but this is not the time to have a two-ton dairy cow following me around. Behind the cow I see Ethan, looking anxious and running fast. Apparently he also knows that the penalty for stealing someone's horse is a big deal.

Once I'm safely hidden in the corn, Ethan catches up with me. I glare at him and make a hissing noise like a cat. "Get away!" I tell him. "You're not my friend! You're trying to get me thrown in jail!"

Panting, he holds a hand up to stop me from talking. "Just listen," he says, trying to catch his breath. He needs to spend more time on his scooter and less time on his MineFarm. I feel fine and I just sprinted the same distance. "Don't panic, and *keep your voice down*. Ms. Tremt knows what she's doing, and we're only here for three hours. It'll be fun! And there must have been a reason she sent us back here to this time and this place."

"You *said* that time travel relies on positive energy and that mistakes happen."

"Yeah, but that was before I knew it was your great-great-great-grandmother's house! That's not

41

a coincidence, Ava. That's deliberate. So let's figure out why we're here! It's a few hours, that's all. Not forever."

I want to run away from him again, but there's nowhere for me to go. A few hundred yards away, I can hear the Pedersen family looking for us. Is this *really* happening? I don't even know how to travel back through the book like he does. I'm totally stuck! Unless I can get Ethan to see reason.

"Listen, Ethan, maybe you're really into all this, and that's fine, but I'm *not*. Today is my big chance—my big opportunity to land a TV job and move to L.A.." I explain all about my audition and what it would mean to me to be able to do it. I make my voice soft and pleading. It's good acting practice for my audition later.

"Does your mom know you're planning to audition for this show and then move to L.A.? Won't she be upset?"

I shake my head. "No, of course she doesn't know. I'll tell her *after* I audition, if I get the part. Which I will. Because I can memorize scripts in, like, five minutes."

Ethan sighs. "Ava, that's not a good idea. And it's not like you at all! You have a great family! Why would you want to change everything and move?"

"You don't understand, Ethan. Your house is so nice and organized and calm. Mine is a disaster every day! I have too many siblings. My mom works too hard. I have too much responsibility. I'm sick of it! And I never get any attention at home. I'm just a pair of hands to help with the little kids or put away laundry. No one cares about me, or asks about me. I want to start over in California, with my dad."

"Maybe things would be better at home if you tried harder to help out more, Ava. You could do more around the house to help your mom and your brother and sisters. That is, if you really wanted to."

I narrow my eyes at him. "Are you saying I'm lazy? Because I'm not. You have no idea how much responsibility I have. You don't know what it's like. Now *I'm* going to go and find a way out of this . . . whatever it is and go home. *Don't* follow me."

I turn and start marching deeper into the cornfields, away from the Pedersens. Ethan doesn't follow me.

Who do Ethan and Ms. Tremt think they are, anyway? They think they know what's best for me. They don't know anything! No one does.

I keep walking in what I think is a straight line, only walking in a cornfield and keeping your sense of direction is totally impossible. There's nothing but rows and rows of corn, taller than my head. I don't even know which way I came from now, because I'm too far in to see Ethan.

Who does this librarian think she is? I wonder. Stranding two *kids* in the middle of the 1800s! At least she gave me my phone. I dig my hand into my pocket to pull it out and check its GPS.

I press the button to call up my location, but nothing happens. There are no service bars at the top of the phone. "NO SERVICE?" I shriek. "That's impossible! How can there be no WiFi on the prairie?"

BOOMF!

Ouch. My temples are aching, like a headache

is about to start. Time travel is really hard on the head. I blink a few times and look around. I realize I'm back in my school library, in the back room. Instead of smelling the sweet prairie grasses, I can smell the day-old odor of a cow having been here.

Phew. No jail time for me. And I probably have plenty of time to make it to my audition too. But what about Ethan? Even though I am still mad at him, I'm worried about him being left back in time all by himself.

The door opens and Ms. Tremt comes in, shutting it quickly behind her.

"Okay, Doctor Who," I say to her. "You've got some 'splainin' to do. I might have to vote you off the island."

"What?" asks Ms. Tremt, who doesn't seem to catch any of the very funny TV show references I just made.

I rub at my temples. "You really need to watch some TV, Ms. Tremt."

"No, Ava dear, *you* need watch *less*."

"Moo!" I look up and somehow the cow has materialized beside me. How did *that* happen?

45

Ms. Tremt smiles. "Amazing. That cow followed you again. You certainly have a way with animals," she says.

"I guess I do. Is Ethan going to appear now too?" I ask. "We were in a bit of, uh, trouble back there on the prairie."

She nods. "Yes, I know. When you pulled out your phone, you left him in the past, Ava, to be captured by Mr. Pedersen. You can't take smartphones back to 1891. You'll terrify everyone! Time travel simply does not allow you to reveal modern inventions to the past. If you try to, *The Book of Memories* brings you back to the present."

Confused, I say, "But you *gave* me my phone! You put it in my pocket yourself. How can I trust you? I don't know what to think."

"Of course I did. I set this all up! It was the only way I could get you to cooperate." She fiddles with her scarf and smiles at me mysteriously.

"You tricked me!" I say. "That's it—I'm looking you up online. I'm going to find out what you really are."

I grab my phone again, relieved to see four bars of service. It feels like a warm hug. I never knew how much I loved cell service. I do a quick search for Valerie Tremt and find . . . zero search results. Zero. Nada. Zip. Zilch.

What is going on? How can a grown woman who has lived thirty or forty or fifty years (it's hard to tell with Ms. Tremt) have *no* results?

"Not everything you need to know can be looked up on your phone, Ava. Some things you need to learn the old-fashioned way," says Ms. Tremt. She goes to the corner of the room and opens a brown box. Leaning over, she digs around inside and pulls out a pile of dowdy brown fabric decorated with white flowers. She brings the pile to me.

"What is that *stuff* you're holding?" I ask. It smells like mothballs.

"Your period costume, of course," she says. "I want you to go back and save Ethan, who is in terrible trouble, by the way, and help your ancestral family," says Ms. Tremt. "I think it's just the adventure you need at the moment."

I don't like this idea one bit. She sent me back to 1891 without telling me, and tricked me into using my phone to come back. How do I know what she's really up to? How can anyone trust a librarian who's really a time traveler? And she dragged poor Ethan into the whole thing too, knowing I'd leave him there! That's pretty crummy.

I lift my chin and glare at her. "And what if I don't *feel* like going back?"

"Then you don't get your phone back," Ms. Tremt says, her hand shooting out and quickly confiscating my phone. "You're not allowed to have this during the school day anyway."

"My phone! Ms. Tremt—*no!*"

"If I were you, and I thought of myself as a good friend, I'd be pretty worried about Ethan right now. Don't you think you owe it to him to go back and help? Horse thieves are not well liked in the nineteenth century. Or any century, really."

She has a point there. If I abandon Ethan, I'll be the worst friend on Earth. And Ethan has always been my buddy. He would go back and save me in a minute.

And maybe it'd be cool to meet my great-great-great-grandma for a second. It's not like many people get the chance to do that.

"Won't my teacher wonder where I am for the field trip?" I ask.

"I can take care of all that," Ms. Tremt says. "I really am on your side, Ava. I promise. Now go get Ethan before he's carted off to jail. And when you come back, you'll see your life very differently."

"Oh, all *right*," I agree, still somewhat reluctant. I'm not looking forward to wearing a period outfit.

I dress myself in the long calico dress, apron, and cap. It's hot and uncomfortable. And then Ms. Tremt tells me I should wear the nano-scarf she gave me earlier on top of it all.

"Just in case," she says.

"This is ridiculous," I grumble. "How do people move in these long dresses? The skirts are totally in the way. And they're *hot*. How come Ethan doesn't have to wear a silly outfit?"

"This isn't his trip."

"Well, then, how come *he* got to go to his dream basketball game on his trip, and I'm headed off to the wilderness?"

Ms. Tremt crosses her arms at her chest and drums her fingers impatiently. "Ethan wasn't the one attempting to audition for a TV show without a parent's permission," Ms. Tremt says.

I gasp. "How do you know about that?"

"I'm a librarian. I know everything. Now, your five-minute modern-device penalty is up. Back you go."

She makes a shooing motion at me and waves her blinking pen. I manage to grab the rope around the cow's neck just as the world around me suddenly dissolves.

*B*OOMF!

"Thief! Vandal!"

I hear these words and some others that must be Swedish and probably not very nice, as I find myself on the ground once again with my head hurting. This time, luckily, I seem to have landed behind a pile of hay, so I'm not out in the open.

An angry man, probably Mr. Pedersen, is yelling now. "You destroyed our fence, stole our cow, let our horse loose, *and* broke the trough!

How could you do so many terrible things to our family?"

Very, very slowly and carefully, I peep around the hay and look for Ethan, who must be getting reamed somewhere nearby. I finally see him sitting on the grass, his hands and feet trussed up with ropes like a chicken about to be roasted in the oven. The Pedersen family is standing around him in a semicircle.

He looks very unhappy and I don't blame him. For a second I'm grateful to Ms. Tremt for making me come back to get him. I'd been thinking about leaving him here to fend for himself, since he's the one with *The Book of Memories* and knows how to get back. But I suppose it's hard to do that when you're tied up and being yelled at by my angry pioneer relatives.

Ethan is red-faced and shaking his head. "I didn't steal anything, honestly! And the fence was, well, I don't quite know what happened to that," he says feebly. I know he's thinking it's probably not wise to explain we fell from the sky because we came through a time-travel portal. That might not go over well.

"You did steal our cow! And we nearly lost the horse, too, because of the broken fence! Shame on you." Now it's Mrs. Pedersen yelling and shaking her finger. She sounds a lot like my own mom.

I wonder why they think Ethan stole the cow. I look around and realize it came back through the portal with me just fine and is munching some grass nearby. But it *was* missing just now. For how long, I don't know. And yesterday when it was outside (and inside) our school library. And then when it came back today, it was in the fields with me as I was running off. So I guess to *them* it might seem like the cow has been gone since yesterday.

Oh boy. That's bad. In 1891, one of the worst crimes imaginable was stealing livestock, especially the kind people relied on for food, like dairy cows. The Pedersen family must need it for milk, cheese, butter, et cetera. Thank goodness I watched so many *Little House on the Prairie* reruns that time I had the flu, or I wouldn't know any of this. But how come I can't remember what the penalty is for stealing a cow or a horse? I'll have to look that up on my phone.

I instinctively reach for my hip pocket, then remember that (a) I'm wearing a long pioneer dress and (b) Ms. Tremt took my phone. I'm completely on my own.

The cow, which is grazing lazily, wanders over to me and gives me a friendly lick, then begins chewing on my apron strings. I don't know if they taste good or if it's just the cow being friendly.

"You're causing a *lot* of *trouble*," I whisper to the cow. The cow looks kind of like she's shrugging and shakes her head. Then she stamps one foot on the ground and looks me straight in the eyes. A long, unblinking stare.

"You're right," I tell her. "We need to save Ethan. But how? What can I say to get the Pedersens to believe he meant no harm?"

"I'm going to have to ride to get the sheriff," Mr. Pedersen says loudly. "You watch him, Laura. Don't let him move a muscle."

I plant my face in my palm. This is it. Ethan needs my help. *Now.*

I decide my only chance is an elaborate act. After all, I have the costume. And I need to be able to act on demand if I'm going to change my life forever and become a famous child star. I might as well start rehearsals now.

"Oh, *there* you are, Ethan!" I yell, making sure to sound relieved, as I come strolling around the side of the mountain of hay. I'm glad to be wearing this ugly old brown dress now. Costumes help build an actor's confidence. "At last I have found you."

The cow, which is clearly one of the smartest cows on the planet, follows me, as I'd hoped she would, and casually grazes beside me. She lets out a soft "moooo," as if to show everyone she's in good spirits and hasn't been harmed.

"Why, hello there!" I call out to the Pedersens, as friendly as anyone can possibly be. "We've been looking for the owner of this delightful cow. My brother, Ethan, and I found it wandering out on the prairie yesterday, and we knew someone must be missing it. So we've been walking for miles and miles, trying to find its owners and do our duty as good, honest citizens. Are you the owners?"

Mrs. Pedersen looks overjoyed to see the cow. Even Mr. Pedersen breathes a huge sigh of relief. "Why, yes, we are, miss. But how in the world did our cow get miles and miles away?"

I shrug casually, as if not particularly worried about how. "Oh, you know, it must have trampled the fence and trough and stormed out. It happens on our farm all the time."

Mr. Pedersen scratches his head. "But the fence wasn't broken until after the cow was gone," he says. "At least, I *think*."

"And the cow is usually out on a picket line during the day," says Mrs. Pedersen. "Not in the stable yard. How could it get loose from the line?"

I glance at Ethan, whose eyes are bugging out because he's so glad to see me. But I can tell something else too—he's impressed. I'm carrying it off. I really am an actress!

"Well, this is quite baffling," I say. "A real mystery. But I'm so happy to be able to reunite you and your cow. And that must be your beautiful chestnut mare over there."

Mrs. Pedersen squints at me. "Yes, that's our horse."

"Now, can I ask why my poor brother is tied up? Did you do that?" I ask Mr. Pedersen, who is still mystified, looking back and forth between me and the cow. Their eldest daughter, who must be Martha, is watching me carefully, while holding two babies in her arms.

No one answers me, so I ask, "Can you let him go, please?"

"Your *brother* broke our fence. And trough. I think. And stole our . . . well, didn't steal, I guess." Mrs. Pedersen is looking slightly confused now too. I seem to have made everyone question whether or not the cow did the damage to the fence. And since the cow and the horse are both present and accounted for, no one really stole anything.

"Of course we can untie him," says Martha. She places the little boys carefully in the grass and then stoops to untie Ethan's knots. As she's doing it, I can't help noticing she looks at Ethan shyly, a small smile on her lips, almost as if she thinks he's . . . cute? *What?* How could my great-great-great-grandmother think that my friend Ethan is . . . *Oooff.* I can't even say it.

I rush over to help undo the knots around his hands and feet. Martha steps back demurely to let me finish, and Ethan gives me a sharp look to let me know he's not happy that I disappeared for a while. *Not my fault,* I want to explain. How was I supposed to know Ms. Tremt set me up with the forbidden phone?

Ethan stands up and rubs at his wrists. He doesn't seem to know what to do next.

"I'm sure my brother would be happy to help you fix your fence," I tell the Pedersens. "He's very, uh, handy."

On MineFarm at least, I think to myself. I elbow him to say something.

"Yes, please let me help you fix it," Ethan chimes in. "And my sister here would be happy to help with the housework. She's wonderful at cooking and cleaning. No job is too difficult for her." He glances over at me triumphantly. "It's the least we can do, since we caused you such . . . inconvenience."

Inconvenience? We found their cow and returned it! And it's Ms. Tremt's fault about the stupid fence. I want to give his arm a good hard pinch, but I know I can't do that in front of the entire family, who are watching us like we might be aliens. I get the feeling he's trying to teach me some kind of lesson, and between him and Ms. Tremt thinking they know what's best for me, I've just about had it.

"That would be very nice," Martha says quickly, smiling at me. She's about my age, and she looks both smart and kind. Maybe we'd even be friends under different circumstances. Like if she weren't my great-great-great-grandmother and I wasn't traveling back in time!

"Are you children . . . orphans?" Mrs. Pedersen asks, looking appraisingly at my slightly gnawed apron and long, loose hair, which probably still has some slop in it from earlier.

I scan the Pedersen children, who, despite living on the prairie with no electricity or plumbing, are all neat and tidy, with clean faces and braided hair and starched aprons. Even the babies look clean.

Think! I scream at my brain. *What can I say to explain our appearance and what we're doing here?*

An American history fact pops into my head. "No, ma'am, we're not orphans. We're . . . scouting land for our parents. They want to settle here . . . under the Homestead Act of . . . 1862."

With each word, I start to remember more and more of that unit in history class last year. The Homestead Act! It's perfect.

"I see," says Mrs. Pedersen. "Well, that makes sense, I suppose."

Awesome. I totally nailed it, and without my phone! I elbow Ethan again, who gives me a discreet thumbs-up.

"You're a bit late, though," explains Mrs. Pedersen sadly. "Many settlers have packed up and gone back East already. Our family came a few years ago, so we had time to plow and get a first crop of corn in. We've worked hard and succeeded . . . somewhat. We just moved out of our dugout and into a real wood house this spring." She proudly gestures toward the tiny house.

I remember that a dugout is a house dug into the ground, with earth for walls, roof, and floor, and sod on top. They're well insulated from the cold winters but often have only a single window for light. Not a fun space for a large family to share.

"Your new house is very nice!" says Ethan,

sounding confused. "But where'd you get the wood siding for the house? There are hardly any trees on the prairie."

"We bought it in town," Mrs. Pedersen explains. "The railroad was put in a few years ago and brings supplies every few days."

I nodded, remembering (also from my history class) that the addition of a railroad back in the 1860s was a huge event.

Mr. Pedersen steps in. "Now, about this fence . . . I know you say you didn't cause it, but nothing like this has ever happened before, and here you all are."

"Like my sister said, I can help fix it," Ethan quickly offers. "Since we've caused so much commotion. And Ava would really like to help you with your chores. To make it up to you."

I glare at him. Why does he keep throwing me under the chore bus? I could have left him here, but I came back to save him! He doesn't seem very grateful. When we get back home and I have my phone again, I'm taking the rest of his MineFarm cows. And maybe his chickens, too.

"That would be very nice of you," Mrs. Pedersen says. "We accept. Martha, you show this young lady how to be useful, all right? But take the babies into the house first, please."

She winks at Martha and heads off toward the clothing line. Martha tells me she'll be right back, and goes to take the babies into the house. As I watch Mrs. Pedersen walk away, she reminds me so much of my own mother that I suddenly feel homesick. I wonder what my mom and siblings are doing right now. Then I realized that in this time, my family doesn't even exist yet. That thought makes me feel more homesick than ever. And it also makes me feel bad about the way I acted last night.

"How much time do we have left here?" I whisper to Ethan.

He checks his watch. "A little more than two hours. Here—hide *The Book of Memories* in your pocket. And *don't* use it without me."

I slide the book into the deep pocket in my skirt. "Thanks for the trust."

"No problem. It's only two more hours, and then I'll make sure we get home, okay?"

"Okay . . . Oh, and by the way, I have an *awesome* idea that's going to make going home a *lot* better. And two hours should be juuuuust enough time to put it into action."

"Wait, what plan?" asks Ethan. "Put what into action? Ava!"

I smile smugly. I can't help it. It's such a brilliant idea that I wonder if it was really Ms. Tremt's plan all along in sending me back to 1891 when I'd asked to go back to 1991. I'd told her I wanted to convince my mom to go to California for college. But what if she doesn't need to be convinced, because the family had already settled there a century before?

"I'm going to get my ancestor Pedersen family to move to California!" I tell him. "If they go now, my family will stay out in California forever. Because why would *anyone* leave the sunny coast? My whole family, every generation, will be born into the good life!"

Ethan shakes his head. "That's not right, Ava. You can't meddle like that."

"But these people are *tough*," I say, feeling my plan is fully justified. "They can make the trip, and it'll be a whole lot easier to live out there than on this prairie, which is probably twenty degrees below zero every day in the winter."

"Ava, you're not allowed to change history for selfish reasons. Ms. Tremt said so. You heard it. You recorded it on your phone!"

I nod. "Yeah, I remember. But it's *not* selfish. It's for the good of my whole family—especially my mom. She'll be happier in California—trust me. Now go fix your fence. I've got some smooth talking to do. And maybe some cow milkin' and hay stackin'."

"Don't talk like a cowboy," Ethan warns me. "This isn't an old black-and-white movie. Don't say *cowpoke* or anything like that."

"Duh, I know. Don't you remember my performance earlier? I got you untied and out of going to jail. This adventure from Ms. Tremt really is amazing. I get to give a better life to a century of Pedersen family members, *and* I get in some acting practice for my new TV career. I'm ready to go in front of the camera! Giddyap!"

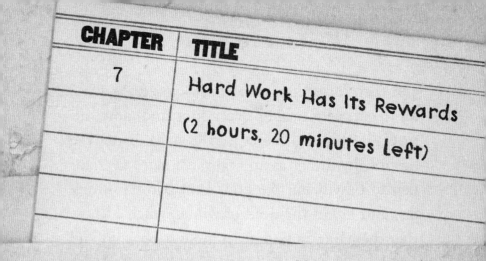

Ethan goes off on horseback with Mr. Pedersen to scout materials for fixing the fence and trough, leaving me to wait for Martha. After a few minutes, she comes back outside without the babies to get me.

"We have to start getting dinner ready," she says. "Would you like to help me with that?"

"Yes, very much," I reply, following her. I keep thinking about what my angle is going to be to get the Pedersen family to consider leaving their new wood house, which they're so proud of, and their large crop of corn. It's going to take a lot to get them to drop everything and move out to California. It'll be especially hard to use the beautiful weather as an argument since we happen to be visiting the prairie on a lovely sunny day and *not* in the dead of winter, when I know that the Minnesota prairies are terribly cold and windy.

In the house, Martha introduces me to another sibling, who is shelling peas at the table.

"This is my little sister, Inga," Martha says, gesturing at the girl, who has two long white-blond braids and looks so much like my sisters Tania and Tess that I wish I had my phone to take a picture. "She's eight and very shy."

Inga's cheeks turn pink and she nods at me, but she doesn't speak.

"Hi, Inga," I say. "I have twin sisters your age who look a lot like you."

Martha tilts her head. "That's funny. Ethan didn't mention he had three sisters when we were talking earlier."

That's because in real life, Ethan has no sisters, only an older brother. I think quickly. "Well, you know how boys are. All he thinks about are, um, horses. And, you know, farming."

"Of course." Martha smiles. "And you already saw our sweet twins, Hans and Jens, who are fifteen months old." The babies are playing in a corner, with just a pair of what look like rolled-up socks as a ball to pass back and forth between them.

Again, I can't help thinking how much our families have in common, even though we lived 120 years apart. Twins do run in families, so I guess it's not that much of a surprise.

"What should we do first?" I ask.

Martha looks me over and then looks at their small and tidy kitchen area, which consists of a cookstove, a single cabinet holding dishes, and a table and chairs. Behind her is a small room with a single large bed in it, and there's a loft upstairs that's open to this main room. There are also two rockers over by the window. That's it in the entire space, and it's all spotless and dust-free.

"You know, maybe before we start cooking we should get you cleaned up," Martha suggests. "You must be hot and dusty from wandering all over the prairie trying to return our cow."

I know she's trying to be diplomatic, and I appreciate it. Clearly I look like I've been rolling around in the manure pile and the Pedersen family can't handle it. "Sure," I say.

She leaves Inga in charge of the twins, and I follow her back outside, where we walk to the water pump. She removes the well cover, which I assume prevents the twins from falling in, and then hands me a bucket. I begin moving the arm of the pump up and down, up and down, surprised at how heavy it starts to feel after a moment and just how long it takes to fill one bucket.

Once we have the bucket of water, Martha makes me lean back and dip my hair into it. "Yaaaah!" I yell.

"What's the matter?" Martha asks, in a worried voice. It felt like she was dipping my hair into a bucket filled with ice cubes—that's how cold it was. But I realized this is probably the way they wash their hair all the time. No hot and cold running water at their fingertips for the Pedersen family. I suddenly miss home even more.

I tell Martha I'm fine; I just didn't brace myself

for the cold water the way I usually do. This explanation seems to satisfy her (thank goodness), and she washes my hair quickly in the icy-cold water, and when I sit back up, I'm shivering and I feel like the temperature has dropped twenty degrees! But I try to act like I have my head washed outside in a bucket of ice water every day, and smile at her as she offers to braid my clean hair for me.

"That would be nice, thanks," I say. Using just her fingers, she manages to comb out my hair, make a perfectly straight part (I've never been able to do that in Tania or Tess's hair—ever), and then somehow pull every single strand of my hair into a braid so tight that my eyelids move two inches closer to my ears. It's pretty painful and certainly won't be falling out anytime soon.

"Thank you so much," I say when she's finished and looking at me proudly. "Want to go for a walk? You can show me around your . . . homestead and tell me about your life here."

Martha smiles wistfully but shakes her head. "That would be lovely, but we must begin preparing dinner! Lots of potatoes to peel."

She hops up cheerfully and heads into the

house, where she hands me a sack of small potatoes and a small, dull knife to peel with.

As I begin peeling, Martha starts measuring out flour and salt and something else, maybe yeast, to make biscuits from scratch. She does it all effortlessly, with no recipe, as if she doesn't even have to think about it.

The small potatoes are round and awkward to hold as I slice off the skins, and I keep losing them. They roll off the table, and Inga quickly retrieves them, while shooting odd looks at her sister.

To distract them from my obvious lack of kitchen skills, I say, "Tell me more about your family. I'm very interested in meeting some more settlers here."

Martha is kneading the dough now, while Inga flours a board for her to roll it out on. It looks so practiced, it must be something they've done many, many times together. Why don't I ever cook with my twin sisters like this?

"Well, as Ma told you, we were some of the first settlers to come here from Sweden. It was very difficult at first. My mother was pregnant with the twins, and Inga was small. We had a terrible first winter here with almost no food." She pauses for a moment and then says, "We had another brother, Elias, who died of a fever as soon as we got here."

Martha stops talking again and looks at Inga, who is staring down at the table. I realize Inga must have been close in age to Elias and still missing him very much. I can't imagine losing a sibling! And to something as simple as a fever?

"Are there any doctors in town?" I ask, hoping that's a normal question. Were there many doctors back in 1891? I can't remember.

"There is one, but we didn't have the money to pay him," Martha says. "Anyway, nothing could be done for Elias's fever."

I do remember learning about typhoid fever running through the country back then, and that while it's treatable with antibiotics now, in 1891 many people did die of it, especially small children or those who were malnourished.

"You are a very brave family," I tell Martha and Inga. "To come here all the way from Sweden! That's an amazing journey. You must be very strong."

As I peel, and Martha talks more about putting in their first corn crop, I examine the house more carefully and really *see* how few belongings this family has. In a house with four kids, there are no toys.

"Um, what do you guys like to play with?" I ask, hoping my question sounds normal. But Martha seems excited to talk to someone new and is glad to tell me everything.

"I have a beautiful box of buttons, and Inga and I made up a game with them. And Inga has a rag doll that Ma made for her last Christmas. We share that sometimes."

As Martha goes on talking about their life, I continue to learn more and more about them. They eat the same foods all the time: biscuits, potatoes, home-baked bread, and whatever meat their dad can find hunting. They get very few fruits or vegetables, except for wild berries and greens. They plan to put in a garden next year. The open loft I can see above the main room is where Inga and Martha sleep, while Hans and Jens sleep in the tiny bedroom off the main room with their parents. Each girl has one play dress and one church dress, and that's it. They have so few *things*. And no chocolate. No candy. No gum. No graham crackers even!

I think about my own room, filled with toys and games and books, stuff I hardly ever look at or touch. Plus all my siblings' rooms and their stuff. Plus my phone, my scooter, our family's computer. Stuff, stuff, stuff, all over my house. And this family has so little.

I become so distracted thinking about everything I have that I stop paying close attention to my work. Martha reaches out a hand to stop me, and I look down.

"You're cutting off chunks of the potato with the skin," she says gently. "But we don't have many potatoes, so we need all of that to eat."

Ashamed, I promise to do better, and even pick up some of the skins with chunks attached and carefully repeel them. How could I waste their food? I feel terrible.

Mrs. Pedersen comes in as I'm trying to fix the over-peeled potatoes. Clearly horrified, she says, "Martha, how about you finish the potatoes and maybe Ava can help with something else?"

73

The twins start crying, and I realize maybe I'd be better off outside with them, where I can do some brainstorming on my plan and not ruin any more of their food.

"I could take the twins outside to play for a bit," I suggest. "I'm very good with babies. Ethan usually does the cooking at our house."

"He does?" asks Mrs. Pedersen.

All of the Pedersen family look at me oddly. Apparently boys do *not* do the cooking in 1891. "I mean, he digs up the potatoes," I say. "And hunts. I'll, um, go get the twins."

I smile and walk over to get the twins, who must be bored out of their minds sitting in a quiet corner with nothing to do, but they seem used to it and are mostly poking at each other.

I gather them up, wondering how on earth I'm going to find the angle I need to make my case for this family to move. I need information. Something to make them understand. On the way out the door, I spy a newspaper carefully folded on the windowsill.

Perfect! That's just what I need. I grab it stealthily and hide it in the folds of my long skirt,

74

thinking to myself that maybe these outfits are sort of useful after all.

Once we're outside, I see that Ethan is now up by the stable, hammering and sawing with Mr. Pedersen, and that my friend the cow is safely tethered to a picket line in a grassy area nearby. I lead Hans and Jens over toward the cow and plop down in the grass. The boys are immediately excited and start to babble at the cow, who very generously moos back at them and flicks her tail, which makes them clap with joy.

Wow. These kids really don't need much for entertainment. My siblings would like to see a cow too, but only because they've never hung out with one before. These kids see the cow every day.

From the house, I hear an exasperated Mrs. Pedersen ask Martha to please hurry up, as they still have quite a bit of baking left to do before dinner, plus setting the table and hauling more water.

Ugh! This prairie life is for the birds. All that work, and the meal isn't even cooked yet. And it's not like it's some fancy delicious turkey dinner either!

I open up the paper, excited to read the news

of the day. The boys are happily pulling up grass and cooing, and the air out here really does smell sweeter than anyplace I've ever been. I suppose the prairie does have the peacefulness thing going for it.

Then I luck out. There's an article on the second page about the railroad. It has recently connected Southern California to the rest of the rail system, making the trip from the Midwest much easier. All they need is train fare, and boom! They're on their way to a much better life.

It's only a matter of convincing them to go.

Really, I'm doing my family a favor in the long run if I get them to move. Look at all the hard work they have to do here! And no toys or neighbors or schools? A doctor they can't afford? Even a broken fence is a calamity.

"If it was this tough to survive on the prairie," I say to the cow, "and you had another option, what would you do?"

"Mooooo!" the cow answers me.

"Exactly," I say. "*Moooove.* I'm going to save this family, Cow. I just need to get ready for my next act."

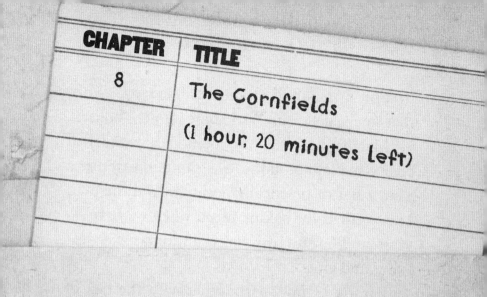

Now that I have my plan for how I can convince the Pedersen family to move to California, it's time for me to put it into action.

"Wish me luck, Cow," I say, as I scoop up Hans and Jens once again and take them into the house. It's all hands on deck now, as the biscuits are rising in the oven and Mrs. Pedersen and Martha are preparing some sort of stinky bean soup on top of the cookstove. My mom makes us rice and beans all the time, which I think taste awful, but something tells me this is a meal they have pretty regularly around here, so I say, "Wow, that smells delicious," as I come into the house.

Martha beams. "My mom is a wonderful cook," she says proudly. "She can pull together a dinner out of practically nothing. And she even knows tricks for baking bread when we have no yeast, and how to season certain things with just leaves and grass."

I think of my own mother with the box of spaghetti and the jar of sauce. No, cooking is not her specialty, but she does heal animals for a living, and she's great at helping with homework. Plus, she's very funny.

Inga comes in carrying a pail of fresh milk from the cow. I'm reminded how glad I am that I was able to return her so they have milk.

"Ava, do you think you could help Martha churn some butter?" Mrs. Pedersen asks me tentatively, as if she's worried I'll ruin that, too.

I decide I can't risk messing up more of their precious stock of food, so I'm honest. "Well, Mrs. Pedersen, our family has just arrived here from back East, where we lived in, uh, town, and so I'm not very good at that yet. But maybe Martha can show me? I'm a pretty quick learner."

Martha agrees, and takes me in the corner with the pail of milk. She strains it and then pours the creamy milk into a large jug. Immediately she begins beating it with a wooden spoon, for what seems like ages, and the milk somehow manages to separate into buttermilk and some other kind of milky liquid with little pieces of actual solid butter in it. She pours that through a sieve and then stows the buttermilk in a cool dark corner and places the butter solids onto a plate and salts it.

Meanwhile, Inga has been setting the table, and Mrs. Pedersen has taken the biscuits from the oven and is now doling out the soup into small bowls.

I can't believe how much work went into just making the bread and butter, things that sit in my pantry and fridge and I grab every single day without thinking about it. And this is just one of three meals they have to make every day! How do they have time to do anything else?

"You all have worked so hard on this meal," I say, without meaning to. It just kind of spills out. "I can't believe it. That's amazing!"

Mrs. Pedersen shrugs and then smiles at her two daughters. "Many hands make light work," she says. Inga and Martha both smile back at her, and I realize that while I've been focusing on all the work and the hows and whys of how all this food came together, the three of them have been happy and chatting and calm, used to their ordinary routine and enjoying each other's company.

None of them are complaining, like my twin sisters would be if they had to do this every day. Inga went out on her own to milk the cow. No one asked her to, and no one had to thank her, nothing! She just did what she knew was her job when she had to do it.

"We're very glad to have the butter today," Martha tells me. "When the cow went missing yesterday, we were certain it had been stolen. It's quite lucky for families in the area to have a cow, and most of the families are so new they haven't been able to buy one yet. If you and your brother hadn't brought our cow back, we would have had a very hard time without milk for the babies, and butter and cheese."

"I love cheese," Inga says softly, which I think is the first thing she's said since I met her.

Mrs. Pedersen nods. "That's true, girls, but remember, we've had worse hardships than a lost cow. Do you remember the year the corn crop was eaten by gophers?"

Inga and Martha nod, and even laugh, remembering how their dad had stalked and hunted those gophers day after day but to no avail. They were too fast and sneaky to catch.

I can't believe it, but I'm actually feeling a little envious of these people! They're all so close, and the kids get to spend so much time just quietly working alongside their mom.

"Ava," asks Mrs. Pedersen. "Do you think you could go out to the pump and bring in one more bucket of water for dinner?"

"Of course," I agree quickly. It's the least I can do, considering what I did to the potatoes, which have since ended up in the bean soup. I run outside and go through the long, arduous chore of pumping up and down, up and down, up and down to get a full bucket of icy water. It seems like only a trickle comes up every time.

With my shoulders and arms aching, I lug the heavy pail back inside and decide I've seen enough. It's time to enact my plan. Ethan and I don't have forever, and I want to help this family have it easier next winter. After being here for just a couple hours, my feet hurt from being bare (most homesteaders wear shoes only in the winter to save shoe leather), I'm sweaty, my arms are worn out, and I can't wait to take out these too-tight braids. Phew.

After I put down the pail of water, I dig into the deep pocket of my skirt, where I had placed *The Book of Memories* earlier. I set the book on the windowsill, so that I can at least be a pound or two lighter. Then I fan out my skirts for a second, hoping for a cool breeze. Prairie clothes are bit cumbersome with all this water-hauling.

I glance around the room, looking for a clock. Ethan is the one with the watch, and I need to know how much time we have left. But there isn't one, so I decide to just jump right in.

"Well, I'm certainly glad Ethan and I found your cow and were able to visit with you all today," I say. "Especially since now I think we

82

can report back to our parents that homestead life is really very challenging."

Mrs. Pedersen looks intrigued. "Oh? Do you think you won't settle here, then?"

"It seems like it's awfully difficult to get a crop started, and then the gophers, as you mentioned, and, uh, all the other things. I think maybe you were right, that many of the families are leaving this area because it's just too hard to make a good life here."

"With hard work and a bit of luck, you can do it," Mrs. Pedersen says emphatically.

I nod, making sure to look around her home and to appear very impressed. "Yes, indeed, you can. But my parents have a backup plan, you see. And I think I'm going to tell them that their *foolproof backup plan* might really be the way to go."

Martha and her mother exchange a look, and Inga stares at me, anxious to hear what I have to say. I stay silent, letting their curiosity build. This is all part of my act. I must make them want *desperately* to know, because then they'll be more likely to think it's a brilliant idea. I learned that on some detective show.

Finally, after what feels like minutes and minutes, Martha says, "Please, Ava. Tell us your plan!"

Slowly I look each of them in the eye. Then I say, "California."

"California?" Martha says. "But it's so far away!"

"Not anymore," I tell her. "The railroad has been running from here to Southern California for a while now, and it's the easy way to travel. You pack up your things, buy a seat, and travel in style. No more covered wagons!"

"But what's different about living there?" Martha asks.

"Less work!" I tell her. "The weather is beautiful and warm and sunny all year round. No hard winters. No starving. You can live near the ocean! It's the happiest place in the world."

"You must work for a good life," Mrs. Pedersen says. "There is no way to avoid it."

"But there are more cities and towns in California," Martha says. "It's more settled than these prairies. Pa and I could get jobs in a town. I can sew for money! Oh, Ma, it could be much easier."

"I don't know," Mrs. Pedersen says. She's begun bringing the food to the table, so I step in to help her. "Nothing is as easy as Ava says it is."

"But, Ma, there would be more doctors there! If we ever had an emergency . . ." Martha lets the sentence trail off, and I know they're all thinking of poor Elias, who passed away. I busy myself wiping the twins' hands with a wet rag from the water bucket and bringing them to the table.

I almost feel a little bad pressuring them like this, but at the same time, I want them to do well! I want them to have a better life.

"You know, if we sold the new house, and the horse, and the cow, I think we could afford the train tickets and have some money left over to start our new life . . . ," Mrs. Pedersen muses. "Maybe it's worth mentioning to Pa at dinner. Just to see what he says."

Martha jumps up. "Should I go call Pa and Ethan in?" she asks.

This is it! I'm convincing them. I can't believe it. Just then, out of the corner of my eye, I see someone waving at me from outside. I assume it's Ethan, but when I look again, I see that the

85

person is taller, an adult, and is he's wearing a dark, modern suit.

What is that all about? Is this another crazy trick from Ms. Tremt, like with my phone?

I need to check it out. ASAP. Maybe this guy was sent to tell us we're running out of time?

"Uh, I'll go get Ethan and Mr. Pedersen for dinner," I offer quickly. "Be right back!"

I run out of the house and scan the fields, unable to find the man again. Then I see a flash of bright green disappearing into the high stalks of the cornfields. What is happening? Where is he going?

In an instant, I decide to follow him. I start running toward the cornfields, yelling over my shoulder as I go, "Mr. Pedersen! Ethan! Dinner's ready!"

I don't wait to see if they go inside for dinner, because I don't want to lose sight of that man. Could he be an ancestor of mine too? But then why would he be in regular clothes?

As soon as I enter the cornfields I can hear him thrashing ahead of me. I try to follow the noise, since it's harder to see in a cornfield than you would think. Suddenly, the cornstalks around me start blowing wildly, moving back and forth like the pendulums on an old grandfather clock. What is happening? I don't remember it being this windy outside when I was getting water.

Then, in an instant, the wind stops. The cornstalks freeze. I see what looks like an open pocket of land in the midst of all the corn and walk straight toward it.

Bizarrely, I step into a clearing filled with what looks like a totally modern house and backyard! It's posh and fancy, with tiny manicured shrubs, a small iron fence, and a *pool*.

Hello, Toto? I don't think I'm in Kansas anymore!

Just as I'm wondering whether I should check out the house or run back to the Pedersen family, Ethan appears beside me, completely out of breath.

"Ethan!" I exclaim. "What are you doing here? I thought I told you it was time for dinner!"

He rolls his eyes. "You did. But then I saw you run straight into the cornfield by yourself and I was worried you were up to something."

"I'm not *up* to anything," I reply, slightly annoyed. "I saw someone out the window. He was wearing modern clothes and waved to me. Then he ran into the fields. I thought he might be a messenger sent from Ms. Tremt or something, so here I am."

Ethan shakes his head. "She doesn't send messengers, Ava! We get the book and three hours to explore the past, and that's it. Then we have to return."

"Well, then, who was the guy, Mr. Smarty-Pants Know-it-All?"

"I don't know and I don't want to know." He glances at his watch. "Yikes! I've been learning so many neat things I completely forgot all about our time limit! Mr. Pedersen showed me how to ride a horse and lasso a steer, although it was actually a barrel we used for practice. It was great! I can't believe you want the Pedersen family to move to California. This is the life."

I sigh, and try to keep myself from strangling him. A half-hour lesson on roping cattle or whatever isn't enough of a reason for Mr. and Mrs. Pedersen and their kids to stay here. They need to go somewhere easier, where they don't have to work so hard all the time.

"Listen," I say, "we don't have time to argue. Let's make sure my plan worked, and then we'll head back to the future. I left the book on the windowsill at the house, so we need to go and get it."

"What's the rush?" says the man I saw earlier, appearing from around the modern house. He's wearing a dark suit and has bright green gloves on his hands. "Thank you for coming, children. I've been anxious to meet you."

Ethan and I stare at the man, our jaws hanging open like we're two goldfish who flopped out of their bowl.

"Who are *you*?" Ethan finally manages to ask.

The man wearing the green gloves smiles, looking both friendly and amused. "Me? Why, I'm Tim Raveltere. Didn't Valerie Tremt tell you about me? We're old friends."

He walks toward us as he's talking and awkwardly trips over a lounge chair by the pool. He catches himself, smiling at us again.

"I've never heard of you," Ethan says, narrowing his eyes.

"Well, I'm a time traveler. Just like Valerie. Isn't that neat?" He uses his gloved hands to smooth the front of his jacket, but one fuzzy glove gets snagged on a button, and he ends up spending a minute extricating the glove from the button, mumbling something under his breath as he does it. He doesn't seem very coordinated for a time traveler.

"So how do you time travel?" I ask, hoping his answer will prove whether or not what he's saying is true.

He holds up one gloved hand and points to the watch on his wrist. "With this watch, of course. I don't have a copy of *The Book of Memories,* but this watch works the same way. Almost."

Slowly, Ethan inches his way over to me until he's standing right beside me. Under his breath he whispers, "Tremt warned me about another time traveler. She said he's always trying to steal her book and that he needs the positive energy generated from our time travel to be able to travel by himself."

My eyes widen as I realize what he's saying. We're stuck in a large Minnesotan cornfield with a . . . sneaky time traveler?

But Tim Raveltere, who apparently overheard what Ethan said, laughs loudly. "Oh, that's jolly. Of course she said that. But she wasn't talking about *me,* children. Valerie and I really are old friends. You have nothing to worry about."

I exchange a look with Ethan. I'm not buying it, and neither is he.

"Listen," Tim says. "I'm trying to *help* you. That's why I brought you here, Ava, to see your mom in 1991! Just as you wanted. This is her house."

"No, it isn't," I say. "This looks *nothing* like my grandparents' house."

"Not the one you know, of course," says Tim. "You changed the past! You convinced the Pedersen family to move. That moment changed the course of your history. So now *this* is where your mom grew up, in sunny California, just as you wished. When you walked into the cornfield, you stepped through my time vortex, and *voila.*"

"Whoa!" says Ethan, looking at me. "You

changed your history! And all I did in 1891 was learn how to lasso a barrel. I need to think these time-travel trips through more before I go."

"Not now, Ethan!" I say. I can't believe I'm actually looking at a *new* life for my family. "I changed the course of history? Really?"

"You sure did," Tim replies. "You can go inside and see your mom if you want."

As I look over the yard again, it all starts to sink in. The palm trees, the flagstone patio around the lovely swimming pool. And is that a security camera? I really did do it! I made everything better forever!

"Come in with me, Ethan," I say, still nervous about going inside. "Tim, you wait out here."

"Sure, sure, of course," Tim says, accidentally kicking a potted plant and spilling some of the dirt onto the patio.

Ethan and I slip in the side door of the house without knocking, as I'm hoping to get a glimpse of everything without actually freaking anyone out. After all, they won't know who we are, because in 1991 we hadn't even been born yet.

The first thing I hear is "Moo!"

Honestly, *again* with the cow?

But it's not a real cow; it's just a sound from a video game playing on the television. Ethan and I peer around the doorway from the hall and see my *mother,* looking like she's maybe in high school, sitting on the couch playing some game. Her hair is pulled up in a ponytail and she's wearing a cozy flannel shirt, despite how warm it is. Something happens on the screen and she cheers to herself as I hear points being scored.

Whoa! My mom likes video games as much as I do. My mom is cool!

The phone rings, and my mom leans across the arm of the sofa to grab a phone on the table.

"Yeah? Hi, Mom. No, I'm playing a video game. When will you guys be home?"

Silence for a moment. Then, "Mom, really? You and Dad haven't been home for dinner for three days. I've been eating by myself every night!" She pauses, then says, "Yeah, yeah, I know there are TV dinners in the freezer. Okay, *fine.* See you later. Yes. Bye."

She hangs up the phone with a *thunk* and puts down her game controller, looking defeated.

I glance over at Ethan. He's looking back at me, frowning. My poor mom. All alone? Every night? She's just a kid! Not much older than Ethan and I are.

Mom turns to the small Yorkshire terrier curled up beside her on the couch. "Well, Moonlight, I guess it's just you and me again. We're always stuck in this house, with nothing to do. We have hardly any yard, and no grass for you to run through. It sure would be nice for us to go live somewhere wide-open and beautiful, like my aunt's house in the country. We could have horses and cows. We could play fetch. . . . There would be lots of space to run around."

My mom sighs loudly as Moonlight yawns and scratches himself with his back leg. "Actually, Moonlight," she says, "you'd probably hate it since you're mostly a lap dog, but man, I'd do anything to go somewhere green and cool and beautiful."

Ethan elbows me. "Your mom sounds just like you!" he whispers. "Only the opposite."

Unfortunately, my mom hears Ethan's voice and freaks out. She turns and sees us watching

95

her. Then, jumping to her feet and grabbing the TV remote, she hurls it at us.

"Attack, Moonlight!" she yells. "Attack!"

Moonlight just sits on the couch and looks at us. He must be an older dog because the fur on his muzzle is gray and he looks bored.

Mom grabs the remote for her video game next and holds it poised over her shoulder, ready to fling it at us as well. "Get out! Get out of my house or I'll . . ."

"We come in peace!" Ethan says, and I whack his arm. What kind of thing is that to say? Although I don't exactly have a plan either. *Hey, don't flip out. I'm your daughter who won't be born for many years* probably isn't going to help much.

We all stand still, staring at one another. Then Mom dashes toward the front door, presses a button on the alarm system panel that makes a rhythmic screeching sound begin, and runs into the bathroom, locking the door behind her.

"THE POLICE ARE COMING," she yells from behind the bathroom door.

"Um, I think we should go," Ethan says.

"It's probably best," I agree. We run back

outside, and I'm sad not to get the chance to see more of my teenaged mom. She seemed so lonely. I forget sometimes that she didn't have any siblings.

We find Tim waiting for us out by the pool, looking eager. I don't have time to wonder why, because the alarm is so loud I just want to get out of there.

We motion for him to run with us back into the cornfields before the police can arrive, although how can the police reach this house while it's inside this bizarre time-travel vortex? Who knows, but I'm not sticking around to find out! I need to get back to the farm.

Once we're safely out of the house, I turn to Tim. "Okay, Mr. Raveltere, now get us out of here! Back to 1891! I need to talk to the Pedersens, *stat*."

Tim looks at me and shrugs. "I can't do that."

Bewildered, I say, "Yes, you can. Of course you can. You brought us *here*. Now take us back *there*."

He nods. "You're right; I did. But you're the one who's in charge of whether or not we can time travel. It's *your* positive energy that makes this vortex work. I can't just wave a magic wand or something." He laughs as if he's said something really funny.

But Ethan and I aren't laughing. "So, wait," Ethan says. "You're telling us that if Ava can't figure out how to be *positive* or do something *positive*, then you can't get us back to 1891, where the book is, so that we can time travel home?"

Tim nods, and Ethan looks over at me. "Oh, yikes."

"Um, how about that we want to go back home? Isn't that positive?" I suggest.

"Nope," said Tim. "You'll know when you have the right idea, because the cornfields will start blowing wildly. That means the travel vortex is opening. Keep trying."

"Oh, good grief. I have to find some positivity in myself to get us back home?" I mumble. "Sure, easy as pie."

Ethan says, "Well, think about why you started this."

"You started this whole thing!" I snap. "And dragged me into it. All I wanted was to be able to give my mom and my whole family the good life. And I thought that if she'd gone to California for college it would have changed everything for the better. But then Ms. Tremt sent us to 1891 instead of 1991. And when we got there, I realized that if the Pedersen family started out in California to begin with, it might make life better for generations. But *then* I saw my 1990s mom—"

"What is the good life, anyway?" Ethan cuts in. "Do you know? Would you really be happier growing up lonely in a house like your mom? She has a pool and nonstop sunshine, like you say you want, but no parents around or siblings or company. And no grass or fields or fresh air like she wants. Do you want that?"

I shake my head no. I can't get any words to come out. I'm thinking so hard about how much my view of the good life has changed now. I thought I knew what it was until I came back and saw the Pedersen family, so cozy in their little wooden house, all working together, relying on their cow and their crops for their very survival, but happy with the simplest things—like a box of buttons. And then seeing my mom in her fancy, alternate-life house. Is that what my life would be like if I went to California and lived with my dad and starred in a TV show? Because it really didn't seem all that great.

"I guess that's not the good life after all," I admit.

"Agreed," said Ethan. "Not even close."

Maybe, just maybe, what I really want is what the Pedersen family has. Time together. Time with my mom. But I don't want to take away everything that made my mom happy growing up. She loves animals, horses, and being outside. That's how she should grow up. Not with lap dogs and TV dinners. After all, the Pedersen family is happy even though their life is hard. Because they help each other. Many hands make light work, after all. I think I finally understand what that means, and it isn't just about getting your chores done faster.

In a flash, I decide I've got to make sure the Pedersen family doesn't go to California. I've got to get them to stay where they are so that my mom will have the childhood she had originally and so I can get back to my family exactly how it was. I don't want to change *anything* about our life, except for how I feel about it.

That's it! The thing that would *really* make our lives better, to give us the good life, would be for me to pitch in more. I can make our house happier, cleaner, more organized, and more fun, just by helping more! Look at Martha. She's my age and she helps her mother and minds the kids and seems happy to be depended on. She helps make everything run there, and she does it with a smile. And she and her mother talk all day and she knows she's valued by the family.

"Back to 1891!" I shout. "I've got to undo what I did. And for the right reasons."

I look over at Tim, and he holds up his wrist to show me his watch, which is now glowing, just the way Ms. Tremt's pen glowed in the library.

The cornfields suddenly begin blowing hard again, and Tim, Ethan, and I start running in the direction of the Pedersen house just as we hear the sounds of police sirens pulling up to the house behind us.

Suddenly I feel a push on my back and go sprawling onto the ground. Ethan lays sprawled beside me. I look up, and Tim has surged ahead, beating us through the corn and quickly disappearing among the waving stalks.

"Did he knock us over?" Ethan asks, rubbing his elbows. "*Ouch.*"

"I think so," I say, picking myself up off the ground. "But why? We're safe. Away from the police. Back in 1891. We're not in any danger, so why push us down to hide?"

"He didn't push us down to protect us," Ethan says. "It was to slow us down. This was his plan all along, Ava! He heard us talking before, and he knows you left *The Book of Memories* behind in 1891. Quick! We have to hurry! We've only got fifteen minutes left!"

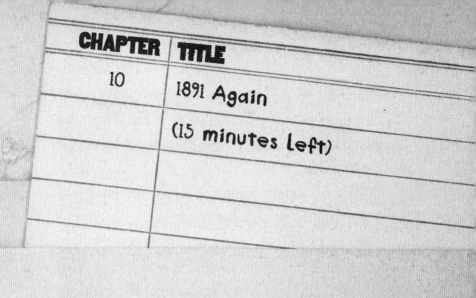

Pretty soon we're right back at the Pedersen's yard, not far from the house. "Where's Tim?" I ask, panicked. We both look around, but he's nowhere to be seen. There is another length of fence knocked over nearby, which is likely his doing. But how did he manage to hop up and run off so fast?

"I guess the more you time travel, the better you get at recovering," Ethan says, as if reading my mind. "C'mon, we've got to beat him to the book or we'll be stuck here forever. And

I *don't* want to fix this fence again."

But just as we start to search for Tim, the Pedersens appear, marching toward us from the house in a line.

"Oh no," Ethan moans. "Here we go again with getting in trouble for the fence."

"We're so sorry!" I shout preemptively, trying to peer over their shoulders and locate Tim Raveltere. I don't see him, but he's got to be hiding somewhere around the house, maybe crouched on the other side, waiting for his chance to sneak in and steal the book. "Let's go in the house and talk about it!"

I say it very, very loudly, hoping Tim will hear me and not risk running in to get the book.

"What are you sorry about?" asks Mr. Pedersen. "This old fence! Bah! Thanks to you, Laura and I and the family have just decided to pick up and move to California! Live the good life. Get work in a town. We're going to sell this place immediately. And the horse and cow. So don't worry about it!"

Mrs. Pedersen is grinning from ear to ear. Then, looking at the fresh damage, she shakes her head and says, "You two seem like such nice children. I can't figure out *why* you keep knocking over our fence. Do you have trouble with your eyes or something?"

Ethan looks over at me and shrugs. I don't know what to do. I know we have hardly any time left, and desperate times call for desperate measures.

"Pedersen family!" I say. "I think you're making a *huuuuuuuge* mistake leaving this beautiful piece of land. Look at everything you've built here! And your corn crop is almost ready to harvest."

"I know," says Mr. Pedersen. "That's why our property will fetch a high price and we can afford the tickets."

"B-b-b-b-b-but," I stutter. "Your dream! You came from Sweden with nothing. You've survived here, on this difficult prairie! And all because you worked together. This is your home now."

Mrs. Pedersen looks at her children lovingly. "Our home is wherever we are all together. The house itself makes no difference. And neither does the land. Home is your family."

Since I just realized that myself a few minutes ago, it's hard to argue with. Especially when they're all beaming at me like they've won free tickets to Disneyland, which they don't even know about, because it doesn't exist yet.

I've got to change their minds. For their sakes! For my mom's sake. For all the generations of my family to come. But how can I do that? What can I say to convince them?

If only I had my stupid phone, I could look up some negative facts about California in the late 1800s. I can't remember *any* except that the California gold rush is already over by now, so they probably won't find gold. But that's not enough to deter them.

Ugh! I need my phone! Wait, do I?

I don't need to have actual *facts* to convince the Pedersens. I can just lie a little. It isn't wrong, because really, they're happy here, and they were planning to stay here before I showed up and ruined everything. So I'm just setting them back on the course they were already on before Ethan and I appeared and messed up their lives. And their fence. With our bad eyes or something.

I just need to think of something scary enough to keep them here.

"Ava," Ethan mutters. "Hurry! I think Tim's inside."

"Okay, okay!" I say. I close my eyes and think hard. Eyes. Bad eyes! That's it! My mind flashes back to an episode of *Little House on the Prairie*, and I realize I have the perfect answer.

"Well," I say, "if that's your decision, I'm happy for you."

The Pedersens cheer and Ethan looks at me like I've lost my mind. Which maybe I have. All I know is it's time to flex my acting muscles again.

I make my face sad and weepy and pretend to wipe a tear from my eye. "I should tell you, though," I begin, "that just before Ethan and I came here to Minnesota with our parents to find a claim, our second cousin, who lives out in California, caught, uh . . ."

Here I pause, as I try to remember the article I read about what *really* happened to Mary Ingalls, Laura Ingalls Wilder's sister, in real life. Suddenly the word clicks, right before my eyes. Thank you, elephant memory!

"She caught meningoencephalitis," I say, "and went totally blind."

"What?" Mrs. Pedersen cries. "Blind?"

I nod. "Yes. Apparently it's a disease that passes easily from person to person. It could be all over California by now. Isn't that terrible?"

Mr. and Mrs. Pedersen look at each other, not speaking out loud but having some sort of serious conversation with their eyes. Martha looks at me, almost suspiciously, as if she knows I'm acting.

Yikes. Could she know? Could she possibly guess what's really going on? She is my great-great-great-grandmother after all. Maybe we have more of a connection than I thought. "That's it!" Mr. Pedersen says finally. "We're staying right here, away from people and their diseases. We don't need any more illness in this family. The Pedersen family will take their chances on the prairie and we'll do just fine."

"Oh, that's wonderful!" I exclaim. "Wise decision."

"Yeah, great," Ethan agrees. "I'm so happy. My sister and I really should be on our way back to our parents now, though. They must be worried about us."

"But first I need to run into your house where I left my . . . handkerchief," I say. "If I come home without it, Ma will be furious."

Martha looks at me, puzzled, and says, "I didn't see a handkerchief anywhere. Do you want me to help you look?"

"Uh, no. Ethan can help me."

I look over at him, and he motions to his watch, the one Ms. Tremt gave him. Oh *no*. We have less than ten minutes. Our time is nearly up!

I dash toward the house, leaving the family to fuss over the fence again. Inside, I look everywhere, which takes only about twenty seconds because the house is small and nearly empty anyway, but I don't see the book. Clearly Tim found it and left with it.

My face falls, and I think about Ethan and me trying to live here forever, growing corn and milking cows. It's like MineFarm, but for real, which means it'll be cold and we might starve.

"Don't give up, Ava," Ethan says, seeing my face. "Let's go look for him!"

He runs out of the house and back toward the cornfields again, the only place around here

109

where a person can really hide. I follow him, hitching up my skirts and moving as quickly as I can.

I can't be sure, but I think I see a flash of Tim's green gloves moving in the corn. "The gloves!" I shout to Ethan, pointing. I'm totally out of breath, and I'm sick and tired of running around barefoot in a long prairie dress. It's like the ultimate workout.

Then we see a crazy bright glow coming from a few hundred yards ahead. It looks totally weird and supernatural coming out of the corn like that. It must be the book, glowing to let us know it's time to go.

"Tim has the book and he's trying to use it," Ethan says. "We've got to hurry!"

We're really down to the wire. We have only minutes left. But as luck would have it, the horse and the cow, both free thanks to us knocking over their fence yet again, happen to be grazing nearby.

"Quick," I say. "You ride the horse! I'll ride the cow!"

"You can't ride a cow," Ethan says disparagingly. "Get up on the horse with me."

I shake my head. I know this cow. I trust this cow. "Go, and Cow and I will catch up!"

Ethan hurls himself up onto the horse's back and gallops off toward the light ahead. I go up to Cow and pat her, saying, "Now, Cow, I really need you to give me a quick ride thataway, okay? Because I've got to get home or my mom will be so worried."

Cow nods and lets me climb onto her back. She sets off at, well, more of a slow trot than a gallop, but it's not bad. We follow Ethan into the corn.

Up ahead, the light is getting even brighter, and I can hear Tim yelling. He's yelling at *The Book of Memories*! "You blasted, dopey, foolish simpleton of a book! Do what I say! I am the boss! You have to obey *me*!"

Cow and I pull up alongside Ethan on his horse. We're behind Tim, so he hasn't seen us yet. Ethan looks gleeful. "The book won't grow for him!" he whispers to me. "It must be because he doesn't have positive energy. Watch this!"

He takes the length of rope he had tied at his hip from his lassoing lesson with Mr. Pedersen earlier and begins to swing it over his head in a big loop. I duck, so that he doesn't take my head off. Then he carefully whips his arm out and casts the loop of rope down over Tim's body, tightening it around his chest and pinning his arms to his sides.

"Brilliant!" I yell. "Ethan, I can't believe you did that. You're the official MineFarm *and* real farm champion!"

"Noooo!" cries Tim, looking longingly at the book, which is sitting open on the ground but not growing a single inch.

"I thought I'd finally learned to make it work!" Tim yells at us. "You children are ruining my plan. I wrote the date and time in it, and I was going to piggyback on your positive energy. I did everything right. You two are messing me up somehow!"

"I guess we are," Ethan says. He ties the end of the lasso to a giant stalk of corn, so Tim can't run off, then slides down off the horse. He goes to the book and carefully writes in *our* return date and time. Finally, the book starts to grow. I'm so relieved I almost can't breathe. I get to go home. Home to my family! Home to a pair of jeans and a T-shirt!

"Ethan," I say. "Tell the horse to go back to the barn so the Pedersens won't worry."

Ethan nods and gives the horse a light slap on the flank. "Go home!" he says, and the horse trots off agreeably in the direction of the barn. I try to do the same thing with Cow, but she won't budge. Instead she stands firmly beside me and rests her chin on my shoulder. She sighs a huge cow sigh and blinks at me with loving eyes.

"Oh my," I say, looking at Ethan. "This cow kind of adores me."

"I guess she can come with us, then," Ethan says. "After all, Ms. Tremt can always send her back through the book later."

"Everybody through the book, then!" I yell. "All humans and, um, bovines."

CHAPTER	TITLE
11	Have Cow, Will Travel

BOOMF!

When I blink, I'm in the familiar back room of the library, looking at the now comforting sight of Ms. Tremt in a fuzzy scarf. Except that her eyes are popping open and her mouth is agape. Then again, we did bring the cow back to the future.

"Oh dear, this is not what I imagined!" she says, looking at something behind us. "Not at all. *Tim!*"

I whirl around and see Tim, still lassoed, trying to squeeze in through the swiftly closing portal.

"Ack! No!" I yell. Then, almost as if she understands everything that's going on, my trusty cow kicks Tim backward, sending him flying back to the past.

"Good cow," I say, patting her. "And fix the fence for the Pedersens, Tim!" I shout through the tiny closing portal. "You owe them that at least!"

When Tim is gone and the portal is fully closed, I turn to Ms. Tremt. "Who *is* that guy?" I ask.

She sighs. "It's a long story, but he's an old time-travel buddy who lost his privileges to *The Book of Memories*. He has a special time-traveling watch, but it's not as powerful as the book. He's always trying to use time travel for his own personal gain. But the rules of the system, which only allow him to travel on others' positive vibes, keep him from making too much mischief. Mostly."

"He was with us on the prairie," Ethan says. "He took us to 1991! And then back to 1891.

We've been back and forth through time a bunch today. *And* I learned to lasso. It was awesome."

"Wonderful!" says Ms. Tremt. "And how about you, Miss Ava the actress? Did you learn anything?"

"Yes, I did," I say firmly. "But before I tell you about it, I need my phone, please."

Ms. Tremt rolls her eyes but hands me my phone. I quickly open up a search window and search for my ancestors on a history website. I scan the results, pleased to see that after a difficult summer in 1891 without their cow, my family bounced back and their farm prospered for generations.

"*Phew*," I say. "The Pedersen family is okay."

"Good," says Ms. Tremt. "But what did you *learn*, Ava?"

It's hard to believe how much I learned during my trip. How could it have been only three hours? It felt like three lifetimes. And, believe it or not, I sort of wish I could do it all over again.

"Well, I learned that my ancestors weren't afraid of hard work. And they weren't afraid of living a hard life, as long as they had one another.

116

And even though we took their cow, which is kind of a long story, they didn't give up and move to California. When I tried to get them to move, deep down I think I knew they'd be happier on the prairie, building their life from the ground up—that's what they wanted in the first place. They enjoy working hard," I say.

I smile at Ethan, remembering that that was what he'd said to me before about why he enjoyed MineFarm. Doing the work himself. Building it from the ground up.

"You really do remember everything," he says admiringly.

"Yep, thanks to my elephant memory. Plus, you know what? I liked doing things on my own—figuring them out without my phone. It was kind of fun. I don't think I'd want to do it all the time, but it felt good knowing I could actually survive without the Internet if I had to. Plus, I learned that I don't want to mess up my mom's childhood. Now I know where she gets her work ethic and her cheerful nature. It's genetic!"

"Well, I am *impressed*," says Ms. Tremt, laughing. "All I meant for you to do was return

117

the cow. According to your family history, the Pedersens' cow mysteriously disappeared during this week in 1891. So I snatched it before it could disappear. I thought it would be nice for you to return it so that your family wouldn't have to struggle and maybe you'd learn a thing or two by seeing a harder life than your own. But it seems events have played out exactly as they were meant to. You did the right thing, Ava. Now, what are you going to do with the cow?"

"Are you kidding? I love this cow! I'm keeping it," I say. "I'm going to wake up every morning and milk it and teach my little sisters to do the same, just like my great-great-great-grandma Martha! And we'll make dinner together and talk about our day. . . . I might even braid their hair. It's going to be great, great, great. Get it?"

"Ha-ha." Ethan snickers. "How about the audition? And your plan to escape to L.A.?"

"Nah, I'd miss my family too much," I say, giving Ms. Tremt a knowing smile. "I'm so glad I went on the trip. I think it may have changed my life forever."

"Time travel has a way of doing that." Ms.

Tremt claps her hands and says, "Now, you kids get home and eat a snack. I bet you're beat. I'll make sure Tim helps the Pedersen family with their fence, Ava, all right?"

I nod happily. "Yes, please. And, Ms. Tremt, thank you. You really helped me."

"It was my pleasure, Ava." She collects our scarves and puts them into a box in the corner, then hands me my school clothes.

She and Ethan leave me alone in the little room to change. It feels so great to take the bonnet off! My head feels light and free, and so do my legs in their cotton leggings. When I come out, Ethan and I wave good-bye to Ms. Tremt in her office, grab our backpacks, and head out to the bike rack to get my scooter.

As we're getting ready to leave, I realize I need to tell Ethan something.

"I might not be able to tutor you as much anymore," I say. "My family needs me after school, and I think they need me more than you do. For a while at least."

Ethan being Ethan, he understands. "Sure, I get it. Text you later?" he says.

"Of course!" I say. "Although I have a feeling I might be too busy to check my phone tonight. I plan on getting my house in order."

"Moo!" agrees the cow, who happily walks alongside me as I scoot on my scooter.

Really, why doesn't everyone have a pet cow? I think they could be the future.

For once, I don't dawdle on the way home. I scoot straight there, because I know that I'm needed. I put the cow in the backyard and latch the gate, hoping she doesn't moo too loudly and disturb the neighbors.

When I walk in the house, our sitter, Bridget, is there. She's obviously just picked up Adam from daycare and Tania and Tess from school, and as usual, backpacks, shoes, and jackets are strewn everywhere. I decided this was as good a place as any to start putting

"Operation Big Sister" into effect.

"Hi, Bridget!" I say cheerfully as I begin picking up jackets to hang in the front closet. "You can go ahead and go home. I'll take care of everybody."

Bridget, a college student with bangs and a silky brown ponytail, looks at me skeptically. At first I feel offended, but then I remember I've never once come home early to help out or told her I could manage things. I've always acted like another person for her to take care of.

"Does your mom know?" she asks.

"Yep," I say. I go to the kitchen, where my mom has the cookie jar with the babysitter money, and pay Bridget for the hour that she worked. She says good-bye to the kids, still looking slightly dazed.

Then I text my mom:

> *I'm home early. Told Bridget to leave.*
> *I'll take care of everything.* ☺

Mom texts back:

> *What about dinner?*

122

I reply:

I said I'll take care of everything!
Don't worry.

I take the rest of the money Mom would have paid Bridget for this afternoon and move it to an empty flour canister. Then I take a piece of paper and tape it to the side, writing *Dinner Dollars* on it. From now on, any money I can save us by doing the after-school babysitting myself, I'll put in this canister and use to order in delivery one or two nights a week, so I can save my mom the trouble of cooking. It's a small thing, but I bet she'd appreciate a nice hot meal she doesn't have to make, until I can teach myself to cook a little bit better. I'm going to download some recipes tomorrow.

I turn to my siblings, who are all looking at me like I have two heads. "Now," I say, "Tania and Tess, your job every day will be to put away the backpacks, shoes, and jackets. I will empty the lunch boxes and unload the dishwasher. Adam," I say, pausing to get his attention. He

123

turns his head toward me and smiles. How did I never notice before how chubby and adorable his little cheeks are? I just want to squeeze him and kiss him.

So I walk over, pick him up, and do just that. I think about poor Martha and her sister, Inga, and how they lost their little brother, and I squeeze him even tighter. "Aaaay-vah," he says.

"That's right, it's me—Ava," I say. "I'm going to help take care of you. Now, *your* job, Adam, is very important. Your job will be to take care of the toy blocks over here, and play with them. Okay?"

I carry him to the corner of the kitchen, where my mom has set up a little play area for him. It's there so she can keep an eye on him while she's cooking. He gets started right away, playing with his blocks and building something with them.

Tania and Tess are doing their jobs, and when they're done, they come back into the kitchen. "Now what?" they ask.

"How about we all do our homework, so that when Mom gets home, we can just hang out?"

They look at each other and nod in unison,

then retrieve their backpacks and plop down at the kitchen table with their books. I give out a small bowl of pretzels and a glass of milk to everyone as a snack, then set up my own books at the table with my sisters. We start doing our work, and when Adam gets restless, I put on his favorite cartoon, and he calms down.

When my mom walks in at five thirty, she stops dead in her tracks.

On the refrigerator whiteboard I've listed our new schedule and chores. Homework has been finished and put away. All clutter has been tidied. I've braided the girls' hair the way Martha did mine (though I didn't do nearly as good of a job), and I'm cooking a frozen pizza in the microwave and making a salad.

"I think I need to sit down," Mom says weakly, collapsing in a chair.

"Are you feeling okay, Mom?" I ask, rushing over to her with a cool, wet paper towel.

She looks at me like I'm a stranger. "What's going on, Ava? Are you about to ask me for something huge? Like a car? Even though you're nowhere near old enough to drive?"

I smile, but inside I feel slightly ashamed that she's so surprised to find me helping out. Was I really so useless before? Expecting my mom to do every single thing just because she's the adult? How did I miss the fact that we are a family and each person helps take care of the others?

Tania speaks up. "Mom, Ava's taking care of everything now. She totally organized us, and made a chart, and we've all done our homework. Even Adam has a job taking care of the toy blocks! Now we can just have dinner and relax."

Mom shakes her head in wonder, and I notice there are tears in her eyes. I hug her, and she hugs me back hard. "I am one lucky mom to have you, Ava," she says. "Lucky to have all of you."

"We're lucky too," I say. "Now, wash your hands and sit down! The twins set the table and Adam did the napkins. Sort of."

We all sit down to eat together, and Mom is so relaxed and happy that I ask her to tell us some memories from her childhood. She's delighted, and begins with stories about her old dog, Moonlight, and how he never left her side, and her horses, and all the riding she did growing up out in the Connecticut countryside.

"It was wonderful," she says. "I wouldn't trade it for anything. Now, how about I do the dishes, since all of you worked so hard this afternoon, and then we can start baths?"

I'm about to agree, when a loud, deep "moooooo" comes from somewhere.

"No phones at the table," Mom says automatically.

"My phone's in my room," I reply. Just then, the "moooo" sounds again, louder, and everyone looks out the window. Sure enough, my cow is standing out there, watching us have dinner. It might be my imagination, but I think she's looking longingly at me. I wonder if all cows are as affectionate as mine.

"Uh, Ava?" Mom says. "Do you want to tell me why there's a cow in our yard?"

"Well, that's a long story. Let's just say the cow found me, and she's very attached, and she doesn't belong to anyone else here. Can we keep her? Please?"

Mom gets up and goes out to the backyard to see the cow. The kids and I follow. Adam and my sisters are totally smitten with her, and pat her ears and moo back at her. She looks thrilled to be getting so much attention.

"I could take care of her, Mom," I say. "And we'd get free organic milk!"

Mom smiles, but she shakes her head. "I'm afraid our neighborhood is not zoned for live-stock, Ava. You have to have a certain amount of acreage."

The cow licks my hand, and I realize how sad I'll be to say good-bye to her. She's taught me so much. And she's so devoted. But she'd be happier somewhere with more room to roam. And maybe some other cows to talk to.

"Do you have a vet client who might want her?" I ask. "Someone who would take good care of her and let us visit?"

Mom thinks a moment, then says, "Why, yes. I do. A family I know just lost their dairy cow and could really use a new one. And they don't live too far away. I could call them in the morning and see if they can pick her up." She studies me. "I'm impressed by your thoughtfulness and maturity today, Ava. I hope it continues."

"It will," I promise. "I know I haven't always been the most helpful member of this family, but I've realized that we need one another and that every one of us is important to making our family work. We might not be trying to survive on the prairies of Minnesota, but we still need one another."

Mom looks at me oddly. "That's funny. Have I ever told you about your great-great-great-grandmother whose family were homesteaders in Minnesota? That was just the sort of thing she wrote about in her diaries. She was about your age when she started writing them. I think your grandparents have them somewhere. I'll ask them to send them to us if you'd like."

Martha kept diaries? Would she have written about a day when two kids wandered onto her farm and broke their fence? That would be awesome.

"Yes, Mom! Please call Grandma and ask her to send them. I'd love to read them. I could even use them for a report at school."

"Okay. I'll call her later tonight. But first, what would you think about getting everyone started on their baths and showers? If we do that now, then you and I might actually have time tonight to watch our show together."

"That'd be nice," I say. "But you know what? It's still light out right now, so how about we all take Sunny for a walk instead?"

Mom gapes at me a little bit, and I don't blame her. Me, suggesting a family walk instead of watching our favorite TV show? It sounds crazy. But TV just doesn't seem as interesting to me anymore. Not with all the other real-life things I could be doing. Besides, after thinking for a while in 1891 that I might not ever see them again, somehow nothing seems better than just hanging out with my family for a little while.

Tania and Tess each grab one of my hands, and Adam toddles to the corner where Sunny's leash is hung up. "Walk!" he says.

"A walk it is," Mom says. "I feel like I'm in dream, Ava. What a proud mom I am right now. Proud of you and your choices."

I can't help beaming and thinking that *this* is the kind of time I really want to be spending with my mom. Not zoning out in front of the TV.

Talking about her childhood, walking together, hanging out with the whole family. This is the good life right here.

I let my cow out of the backyard so she can walk down the street with us. "She won't run away," I tell everyone. "She's a very loyal cow."

And Cow, sure enough, sticks close by my side as we do a loop around the neighborhood. But I start to think about the Pedersens. Maybe I *will* return the cow after all. I'll talk to Ms. Tremt about it. The twins talk to Mom about their day, and Adam rides on my hip, happily clutching some of my hair in his fingers.

As Mom and my sisters walk ahead, I suddenly see a shadow pop up from a bush to my left. It's not a shadow, though; it's the Viking I saw yesterday.

He shakes his finger at me and says, "That's *my* cow. I stole it fair and square."

I squeeze my baby brother with one arm and hold tight to the cow's leash with the other. I flash the Viking a huge grin. Maybe I will return the cow, but for today at least, she's still mine. "Me too," I say. "Go find your own."

IF YOU LIVED IN
AMERICA IN 1891 . . .

For three hundred years, from the 1600s to the 1900s, settlers spread across the vast lands of the new world, beginning with the settlements in Virginia and Massachusetts. Beyond the Appalachian Mountains were wide, fertile lands, and many families from New England and the South moved west in search of flatter, less rocky land. Immigrants from European countries, including England, Wales, Scotland, Germany, Norway, and Sweden came to the frontier, believing it offered political freedom and economic opportunities they couldn't find at home. The Homestead Act of 1862 gave any adult the chance to own their own land and support themselves.

Many people came nearly empty-handed to the frontier. They traveled by covered wagon and usually had only an ax and a rifle, if they were lucky. Some had small pieces of furniture and bedding with them, or farm tools. Some brought seed to plant crops. But along the routes west, many found disease, starvation, and danger. Some families failed and returned to the East, where they had relatives and could scratch out a living in the cities.

Those who stayed on the prairies farther west had to be strong and self-reliant. In most areas, there were no stores or towns yet to buy supplies, so they had to make everything they needed, using the resources that were available. They built lean-tos and shelters from wood, or made dugouts (houses dug into the ground) to live in. They relied on their neighbors, when they had them, to trade goods or share coals from their fires. The families often had many children, in order to help with the workload on the farm, including chasing animals away from the crops, chopping wood, tending the fire, cooking, spinning, sewing, and mending.

THE HOMESTEAD ACT OF 1862

The Homestead Act was signed into law by president Abraham Lincoln in May of 1862, after the secession of the Southern states. It remained in effect for more than one hundred years and has been called one of the most important pieces of legislation in the history of the United States. It encouraged Americans to settle in the western half of the United States by allowing them to put in a claim for up to 160 acres of federal land for free. Any adult who headed a family or was twenty-one years of age, including freed slaves and single women, was eligible. To "prove up" on the claim, one had to pay small registration fee, build a home on the land, and live and farm on it continuously for five years. However, a settler could obtain the land after only six months' residence if he was willing to pay $1.25 an acre.

More than fifteen thousand homestead claims had been established by the end of the Civil War, and more followed in the postwar years. Ultimately, 1.6 million individual claims would be approved.

Pssst," I whisper to the girl sitting in front of me. Maria Malki flips her long, bouncy brown hair, then turns around and stares at me, her black eyes looking like they will shoot flames if I dare make another sound. She puts her index finger on her lips and hisses, "Shhh, Kai!"

I twist my face so it looks like one of those super-sad clowns you see in the paintings at a mall stall. Maria's stony look starts to show a few cracks. Her lips turn up a teeny-tiny bit at the corners. I see a sliver of opportunity, so I decide that I'm definitely going to squeeze my way in.

Maria's a rule follower. I get that. I'm a pretty straight-and-narrow kind of guy myself. I've only had detention three times this year, and two of them weren't even my fault. But I admit that I'm not above bending the rules a little. Especially when it involves getting a laugh or two. I *live* for laughs.

The rule Maria is reminding me about is "No talking during Mr. Bodon's math class." He's pretty strict about it, and breaking it already got me the one detention that I actually deserved.

But Mr. Bodon just left the room to go talk to Principal DiBella, and I desperately need to try out some new comedy material, so here goes nothing. . . .

"Hey, Maria," I whisper. "What's blue and smells like red paint?"

Maria is *not* going to break the rule and answer me, but I can tell she's all in when she turns around and shrugs her shoulders to let me know that she doesn't know.

Katrina, Jaden, and Faris are sitting close by, and they're all in too.

"I don't know. What?" Faris whispers.

"Blue paint," I say matter-of-factly.

Maria drops her head on her desk and groans. My friend Matt snickers from two rows over.

"Dude, that is such a dumb joke." He laughs. "Did you actually spend time coming up with it?"

"Did it make you laugh?" I ask.

"Well, sure," Matt says. "Because it's soooo dumb."

"Doesn't matter," I say. "If it made you laugh, it worked."

Maria's head is still on her desk, but I think I can hear the faintest sound of a giggle. Success!

Mr. Bodon comes back into the room and starts writing math problems on the board.

"You have ten minutes to complete these problems," he announces to the class. "If you need help, come see me in the consulting corner."

Mr. Bodon's "consulting corner" is a card table with two chairs that he put in one corner of the classroom. It's kind of cheesy, but he's actually one of our coolest teachers. I start writing down the problems he's written on the Smart Board and I can tell that I'm going to need some consulting with problems two, three, and four.

I finish writing the problems down and I'm just about to close my notebook and head to the card table when a folded piece of paper lands on my desk. I open it and see that Maria has written the formula for figuring out the perimeter and area of quadrilateral shapes on it. Now I can do all the problems on my own. Sweet!

It's probably a good time to explain that Maria Malki has been sitting in front of me for five years now. We went to the same elementary school, and since my last name is Mori, alphabetical-order seating has pretty much doomed us to being friends. She knows that I never remember to bring my sheet of math formulas, even though I'm supposed to. I know she's one of the best students, and artists, in our grade.

I guess "doomed" isn't really the right word, though, because even though we're really different, like, opposite-ends-of-the-spectrum different (and I'd never admit this to my guy friends like Matt), I think Maria is kind of cool, for a strictly-following-the-rules-kind-of girl, that is.

Thanks to Maria, I finish the math problems in four minutes, so I have six minutes to let my mind wander. I should probably start working on a new joke, but I'm not really in the mood, so I just look down at the floor in front of me, which is where Maria's stack of books and her backpack are.

Another thing about Maria: She is obsessed with animals. I've never seen her room, but I'm going to guess she has posters of kittens and tigers and dolphins plastered everywhere. She's probably drawn a lot of them too, because she's a pretty amazing artist. Her backpack is covered with bubble-pen drawings of animals that she did herself, and it actually looks like something you could buy in a store.

I don't even realize it, but while I'm looking at the backpack, I start doodling in my math notebook. Inspired by Maria, I guess. Stick figures are about the best I can do, but I get distracted pretty easily, so I've always liked to doodle because it helps me focus when my brain would rather be somewhere else. I start with some swirly waves and then add some dolphin fins and starfish, simple stuff. I get so absorbed in it that I'm totally startled when the end-of-period bell rings. I jump up and accidentally flip my notebook off my desk.

Maria is already packing up her stuff, so she grabs my notebook and sneaks a peek at my doodles. How totally embarrassing! She's a real artist. I'm a . . . a doodler. And not even a decent doodler. Ugh. She's totally going to laugh at me. And not the kind of laugh I'm looking for.

"Here, Kai," Maria says, handing me the notebook.

Wow, not even a smirk. Amazing!

Then she quietly zippers her backpack and starts to head off.

"Uh, thanks, Maria," I call after her. "See you at lunch!"

Maria turns around and doesn't even lift her head when she says, "If you really care about ocean creatures, you should come to the Be the Change club meeting later."

"What was that about?" Matt asks, shoving me in the back. "'See you at lunch!' Is there something you're not telling me, Kai?"

"What? No, nothing!" I protest. "She just helped me, so I figured I had to be nice. I'm not rude, Matt!"

"Of course you're not." Faris laughs. "Just ignore him."

Faris turns to Matt and says, "Come on, like Kai would ever like Maria! She's so quiet—and he's so loud!"

Matt laughs. "Yeah, you're right. Kai would just bulldoze every conversation."

"Gee, thanks, guys," I say. "It's nice to know you really appreciate me."

"Aw, don't take it personally," Faris says. "We love you. You're our favorite class clown ever!"

I should be more upset than I am, but I'm not really paying attention to them anymore. I'm thinking about how I'm going to come up with some kind of sea creature joke before the Be the Change club meeting.

When I find Maria in the cafeteria after school, she and Jada are waving their hands while they talk. It's a girl thing. I decide to watch them for a few minutes. I like to study people's expressions and gestures. It helps with my comedy routines, if I can mimic them closely. Like, watching Maria and Jada right now, I'm pretty sure I can get a middle-school-girl impression down pretty perfectly. I get a little closer so I can hear what they're saying, but they're both too focused on the conversation to notice me anyway.

"We could have a bake sale to help a local shelter," Maria says. "Or maybe a poster contest to show why it's important to help save the animals of the rain forest? Or . . ."

"Those are great ideas, Maria," Jada says. "But right now we're all tied up with toy drive for the children's hospital. I don't have any time to spare."

"Well, if you start an animal-charity subgroup," I suggest, "you won't have to spare any time. Someone else will."

Jada and Maria whip their heads around and stare at me.

"When did you join the club?" Jada wonders.

"Oh, I asked Kai to stop by," Maria said. "The more the merrier, right?"

"Right." Jada laughs. "So are you going to lead this subgroup, Kai?"

"Um, I think that sounds like a job for someone a lot more together than I am," I admit. "Like Maria?"

"I'm in," Maria says.

"That would be great, if you can to take total

charge of it, Maria," Jada says. "I'm trying to not make myself crazy with this stuff."

"I can," Maria says. "With Kai's help, of course."

"Of course." I laugh, hoping my cheeks aren't turning red. "But I have to go now. I've got plans . . . you know . . . um . . . this thing . . ."

"Right," Maria says. "Why don't you just stop by my house when you're done and we can brainstorm some ideas?"

"Sorry, I think this, um, thing is going to take a while," I say cryptically. "Can we meet tomorrow? At the library maybe?"

"Sure," Maria says. "I'll make a list of some ideas tonight and bring them with me."

"Great!" Jada says, already whirling off to talk to another group of kids. "Good luck, you guys."

"See you tomorrow, Kai," Maria says, smiling. My eyes lock in on her teeth. They're perfectly white and straight. I've never actually noticed that before, and it makes me remember my mouth full of metal braces. I put my hand over them and mumble, "Bye."

At home I finish up my homework quickly. Writing comes really easily to me, so the five-page social studies paper that everyone's been complaining about takes me only about an hour to finish, and then I spend another half hour on math and science. Then it's time for my real homework. Comedy!

So none of my friends at school know about this (and don't tell them!), but I entered a comedy contest that WKBL, our local radio station, is running. I have to prepare a five-minute stand-up routine to perform at the Smoke Eater's Jamboree (a festival to raise money for our fire department). I'm doing a "Did You Ever Wonder Why?" theme. It's full of lines like, "Did you ever wonder why we sing 'Take Me Out to the Ball Game' when we're already there?"

My mom is the funniest person I know—no joke!—and she's been helping me get ready, but I want to write at least another page of jokes. That's the thing about comedy. You have to write a lot more material than you need, so that you can cut the stuff that doesn't really fly and keep only the best stuff. I'm not sure about the "Take Me Out to the Ball Game" line, but I'm going to try it out and see if it makes anyone laugh. Mom first, of course, because I know she won't let me embarrass myself out there. Besides being funny, she's brutally honest, too.

Dad's the first to get home, and before he even says hello to me he turns on the rice cooker in the kitchen. You might have guessed from my name that my family's originally from Japan, so rice is part of dinner pretty much every night. Our rice cooker has probably made enough rice to fill one of the Great Lakes.

Pretty soon Mom's home, and I run some of my new routine by her.

"Did you ever wonder what it would sound like if Kermit the Frog rapped?" I ask.

I do my best impression of Kermit the Rapper.

"Cute," Mom says. "But don't you think the Chipmunks would be funnier?"

Right! My Chipmunk impression is killer. I start to rap again, but this time with a super-squeaky voice.

Dad snorts and Mom laughs at him.

"Do I know funny?" she asks.

"You know funny, Mom," I agree.

Dinner's ready and the table's all set when my big sister, Yumi, and her best friend, Val, come bouncing in the door. They're on the high school gymnastics team, so when I say bounce, I mean it literally.

"How's good old Sands Middle School?" Val asks, snickering.

"Probably the same as when you went there," I reply.

"I'm sorry," Val says.

"It's okay," I say.

Yumi and Val start talking about this boy they know who used to go to middle school with them.

"Have you seen Troy Mendez?" Yumi asks.

"OMG!" Val screams. "When did he get so cute?"

"Does he still have braces?" I ask.

Yumi and Val both look at me like I have six heads.

"What?" they say.

"Does he still have braces?" I repeat. "I mean, can he be cute with braces?"

"No. He got them off last year," Val says.

"Why, are you hoping someone thinks you're cute with braces?" Yumi teases.

"No. I was just . . . um . . . wondering," I stammer.

Thankfully, the phone rings and interrupts our conversation. It's Oji-san, otherwise known as my uncle Kenji. He lives in Honolulu, Hawaii, which is where my mom grew up. Oji-san is a lawyer, just like my mom, and once they get started talking, there's no stopping them. We finish dinner and clean up and Mom is still on the phone, asking a ton of questions all about her brother's new case in Hawaii's environmental court.

I head up to my room to escape from Yumi and Val, and check my cell phone. (We're not allowed to have phones at the dinner table—strict Mori-family rule.) There's a text message from a strange number. I tap on it and see: *Hey! Library tmrw still cool?*

It's Maria! How did she even get my number? I agree to meet her—of course—but figure I should do some research before I go to bed, so that I'm totally prepared for our meeting. I start digging around Oji-san's cases with the environmental court, because I know he's done some work getting wildlife protection there. It's kind of a family tradition, actually. Baba, my grandmother, is a marine biologist. She's studied the breeding cycles of the local fish schools and helped make sure that endangered species weren't overfished. Maria is going to be soooo impressed!